MW00649626

Sebastian Michelson was born and raised in Queens, NY. Michelson has always loved music since he was a little boy and would sing along with the recordings of his favorite singers. Michelson studied voice and sang in church and community musical theatre productions for several years. Michelson still lives in Queens with his family and works in the university system while pursuing a master's degree in Spanish. When he is not working or singing, Michelson loves to bike ride, power walk, journal write and is an avid dog lover. Faith and family are paramount to Michelson.

.

This book is lovingly dedicated to the Lord who is truly my Father and to my mother, Miriam, and grandmother, Dorothy; the two strongest and most loving women I know. RIP with the Lord and your guardian angel, Gloria… Grandmama.

Sebastian Michelson

VINCERO... I WILL WIN!

AUSTIN MACAULEY PUBLISHERS™

LONDON • CAMBRIDGE • NEW YORK • SHARJAH

Copyright © Sebastian Michelson 2021

Ordering Information
Quantity sales: Special discounts are available on quantity purchases by corporations, associations, and others. For details, contact the publisher at the address below.

Publisher's Cataloging-in-Publication data
Michelson, Sebastian
Vincero… I Will Win!

ISBN 9781649793331 (Paperback)
ISBN 9781638299394 (Hardback)
ISBN 9781649793348 (ePub e-book)

Library of Congress Control Number: 2021915502

www.austinmacauley.com/us

First Published 2021
Austin Macauley Publishers LLC
40 Wall Street, 33rd Floor, Suite 3302
New York, NY 10005
USA

mail-usa@austinmacauley.com
+1 (646) 5125767

I would like to thankfully acknowledge Austin Macauley Publishers for taking a chance on a new author like me.

Chapter 1

"Vincero... I will win!" This line has always been quoted to me by Grandmama Rita and sung to me by Luciano Pavarotti. If only I could turn back time. How many times have we all pondered that age-old question? What would we do differently? What choices would we make? Whom would we love? What profession would we have? These are all honest questions I believe we all ask ourselves. I know I certainly have during my turbulent time on this Earth.

Allow me to introduce myself. My name is Sebastian Devereux, and I have just recently turned 41, and I am now at the pinnacle of my singing career as an opera singer. I have what some would describe as "having everything I want" yet there still remains a longing, an empty void that needs to be filled, or perhaps it may be a great need for a change in direction but would that look like? Do I need a change in personal relationships? Would I need a change in career? Oh Lord, pray tell what must be changed in my life? How did I end up here in the present day as a gainfully employed opera singer after so many years of studying, waiting, and persevering to truly end up in this unexpected reality? You may all ask why I say "unexpected"? I guess I am also asking myself that same question. Here is my story.

A young early middle-aged man with dark brown wavy hair who stands at 5'9" tall wearing a dark blue suede sport jacket, blue and white pin-striped shirt neatly tucked into his black belt and black jeans and maroon red penny loafers walks on stage standing fully erect to be greeted by applause and the uniformed rise of musicians warmly greeting their featured soloist. An elder statesman-like figure enthusiastically yells "BRAVO... BRAVO" as this featured soloist politely but sheepishly received this warm reception by all present company.

After all the applause and cheers have died down, a brief silence occurs. The maestro commands the orchestra to then play *Federico's Lament*; we then hear the opening bars of a tenor aria playing. The aria is called *E La Solita Storia* written by the Italian composer Francesco Cilea, and it is a lament from a very unhappy shepherd who is being forced to marry a woman he does not love only to please his family. Yet the woman, Vivetta, whom he is supposed to marry loves him with great feverish abandon. This is what you would call unrequited love at its most powerful. Still, Federico, the shepherd, loves this other girl *L'Arlesiana* who is only called a girl from the town of Arles and ponders over the letters she has written to him.

As Sebastian begins singing, he feels chocked up and can barely sing the aria only to have to stop himself and the huge orchestra along with him midway through the second stanza. The conductor Maestro Fulgencio looks horrified but approaches Sebastian in a very paternal and nurturing way so as not to overwhelm him even more:

"Sebastian, my dear man, what's the matter? You were singing so beautifully until you choked up in the middle of the second phrase? Is everything alright?" asked Maestro Fulgencio in a soft-hearted caring way with his notable Italian accent.

Looking like a deer caught in headlights, Sebastian responded, "Maestro I'm sorry… I am so incredibly sorry. I don't know what has come over me. Maybe we can start over? I don't know… I just don't know."

Maestro Fulgencio looking with great concern and tender loving care at Sebastian knew that Sebastian would not be able to go on at least not at today's rehearsal has decided to take matters into his own hands and do what was best for Sebastian and the whole company at large.

"No, my dear Sebastian. I think it is best for you to stop here for now. I want you to go home and rest, and we will talk on the phone later."

Maestro Fulgencio then turned to the orchestra and said, "We will table *Federico's Lament* for another day as Mr. Devereux is indisposed and can, therefore, not go on today. We will pick up with Mr. Di Lorenzo's baritone aria the *Toreador Song* from Carmen by Bizet!"

As Jonathan Di Lorenzo approached the stage to assume his position, he looked out at Sebastian in a very concerned way as both he and Sebastian have become very good friends and have often sung together in various operas and voice competitions. Jonathan and Sebastian looked at each other briefly and then nodded as the music for Jonathan's aria played, and Sebastian exited the hall.

Sebastian exited the concert hall of the Civic Center in New York and as was greeted by a darkening stormy looking sky; he felt it was reflective of the inner storm taking place within him. Sebastian began to ponder on the recent loss of his beloved grandmother Rita who practically raised Sebastian or Seby as she lovingly referred to him while he was growing up. She was very much a strong, loving, and nurturing figure in his life.

Rita has just recently died from cancer and lived to be 88 years old. She had so much tenacity and zest for life that one would assume she would have lived to be at least 100 but as Sebastian and others have come to discover that even the strong and tenacious all succumb to death sooner or later.

Sebastian now entered his car, and as he drove away he turned on the radio only to be greeted by the powerful opening bars of the song *Gloria* sung by Laura Branigan. What made this so powerful was that Rita had named her guardian angel Gloria two years before she died. Rita would often share with Sebastian and his mother Vanessa that she could see a female guardian angel everywhere guiding her as she went about her life even before she was diagnosed with advanced Stage four Cancer six months before she died.

The song started to play 'Gloria... Gloria... Gloria'. Now if you listen to the lyrics, one would wonder what they possibly had to do with Rita, but Sebastian thought it was Rita's way of just trying to tell him she was fine now in Heaven with God and his grandfather, Nick, or Poppy *Rocco* as he was more lovingly called in his youth.

"Grandmama, is that you trying to call out to me?" As Sebastian started weeping as he heard the song play it suddenly dawned on him that Gloria was his grandmother Rita's angel's name; therefore, it must now be her new singing calling card to him.

"As nice as this song is to listen to I think I have a more appropriate song or aria in this case that you might like better." Sebastian took out a Luciano Pavarotti CD of famous arias and played the last track famously titled *Nessun Dorma.* As Sebastian drove on the Queensborough Bridge, he raised the volume on the radio to be greeted by the climactic final stanza leading to the final victory cry of *Vincero... Vincero* which means I will win... I will win! Sebastian welled up with tears but then bravely took out his handkerchief to dry his eyes as he knew he needed to get home safe and sound to his apartment in Bay Terrace in Northern Queens.

Sebastian finally arrived home, and as we looked into his apartment, we saw a beautifully decorated early American apartment lovingly adorned with a beautiful cherry red dining room set and china cabinet on the right with two steps leading up to it. Everything looked brand new as it had never been used before. Sebastian decided to spend some time on his terrace but, before he did that, he played his answering machine only to find a message from his loving mother, Vanessa.

"Hi, sweetheart. It's mom. I know you're out but just wanted to make sure you're okay. Just remember grandma loved you very much and would want you to go on with your life as her brave and handsome Seby. The weather is beautiful in Sarasota today! I'm going shopping with your aunt Valeria as she is visiting me from Kissimmee. She has decided to spend a few days with me since her family went on vacation for a week. Okay, sweetheart, call me back when you can and always remember... I love you very

13

much and so does Grandma Rita," voice mail message ended.

A second message came on the machine, and it was from the office of a Matthew Porter. "Hi, this is Matthew Porter. I'm a freelance writer and would very much love to set up an interview with you as I would like to do a biography on you as I want to write a book on your life. I hope to hear from you so we can set up a time to meet. My # is 347-555-3377. I look forward to hear from you soon, Mr. Devereux. Bye for now," said Matthew cheerfully and hung up.

Sebastian looked bewildered as he walked toward the terrace, and as he looked out, he sat down and played some relaxing harp and piano music on his mini stereo box as he sipped a nice cool glass of iced tea as he reflected on his life as the afternoon sunset could be seen reflecting on Little Neck Bay after the heavy downpour that had just fallen. Sebastian closes his eyes as he meditates upon the relaxing music that plays in the background.

Two hours pass, and Sebastian waited for his dinner to be prepared by his housekeeper Mrs. Alba who was a sweet-natured lady 50ish with blonde hair and buxom built. She prepares one of his favorite dishes, angel hair pasta with grilled chicken and veggies. She is married but has no children; therefore, she can devote more time to working for Sebastian and his mother when she is in New York.

"Mr. Sebastian, how are you feeling today? How was rehearsal today?" asked Mrs. Alba as she served Sebastian his meal at the dining room table with an interested smile.

"Ah, my dear, Mrs. Alba. It was a rough rehearsal, at least for me anyway, As I was singing *Federico's Lament*,

I choked up midway through the aria. Maestro Fulgencio bless his heart couldn't have been more supportive, but even he realized the show must go on and asked me to leave rehearsal so I could take a rest," said Sebastian frustratedly and sighed.

"Oh, I'm sorry, Mr. Sebastian, but you will be fine. Remember you have been through a great deal lately. You just recently lost Mrs. Rita, and that can take a toll on anyone let alone a sensitive artist like you, and I know Mrs. Rita is watching over you. This too shall pass, but you need to give yourself time to grieve. Why don't you take some time for yourself to work on something to help you process all of this?" said Mrs. Alba in a concerned way.

"Mrs. Alba, I know you mean well, and you're the only other one apart from my mom and grandmama I would listen to, but how can I possibly take time off? This concert is in two weeks, and I need to be ready. I don't want to drop out as I need to sing. I want to sing!"

"I'm sure if you explained things to Maestro, he would understand. You only gave yourself three days to mourn. Maybe you need a longer mourning period, Mr. Sebastian?" asked Mrs. Alba.

"Well, I am not going to think about it right now and will enjoy this wonderful meal you have just placed before me," said Sebastian forcing a small crooked smile on his face.

"Now that's what I like to hear, my dear Mr. Sebastian." Mrs. Alba left Sebastian to enjoy his meal in peace and turned on the stereo as it played classical background music.

An hour later, the phone rang and Mrs. Alba picked up the phone to hand it to Sebastian.

"Mr. Sebastian, your mother is on the phone."

"Thank you, Mrs. Alba," replied Sebastian.

"Well, my husband is downstairs waiting in the car for me. I'll be leaving for the night. I'll see you tomorrow. Have a good night, Mr. Sebastian."

"Thank you for everything, Mrs. Alba. I'll see you tomorrow. Have a good night, and please send my regards to Mr. Alba."

"Yes, I will. Good night," said Mrs. Alba.

"Hi, mom, sorry I was saying good night to Mrs. Alba," said Sebastian.

"Did you get my message? I know you were busy today at rehearsal, but I just wanted to see how you were feeling," Asked Vanessa.

"I'm fine, mom. Just finished having supper. How's Sarasota? How is Tia Valeria?" asked Sebastian.

"Oh, she's fine. We went shopping at the farmer's market, and we then went to some outlet stores, and finally, we went to the UT mall," said Vanessa.

"That's good. I just can't believe she's gone," said Sebastian, referring to his grandmother Rita very solemnly.

"I know. I can't believe it myself. She was vibrant, strong, funny, and she kept everyone going," Vanessa started tearing up as she said this.

"I know, Mom. Just know she cared for you very much. And I'm glad you both remained close well after the divorce with my father."

"Yeah, me too. I think she realized that I would never have stopped you from seeing her or your grandfather, Rocco. They were like second parents to you and loved the relationship you had with them. Not a lot of kids and grandparents do."

"Yeah. Mom, I'm going to hang up now as I want to do some spin biking and shower and then get ready for bed. I love you, and please send my love to Tia Valeria," said Sebastian.

"Alright, sweetheart. Have a good night. May God be with you! Just remember, I'll be coming home next Friday."

"Okay, I'll pick you up at the airport but in the meantime enjoy your time with Tia Valeria, and we'll talk soon. Love you and may God bless you too," said Sebastian and then hung up.

After Sebastian hung up, he received a call from Maestro Fulgencio Riccardi. Sebastian answered the phone.

"Hello?" asked Sebastian.

"My dear Sebastian, how are you feeling? I know you left terribly upset during rehearsal today?" asked Maestro Fulgencio very concerned.

"I'm alright, Maestro, and I'm sorry about today. But I need more time to mourn my grandmother's death," replied Sebastian.

"I agree, Sebastian, and want you to take a short leave. The concert won't be for another 3weeks. Take some time for yourself. Why don't you travel to meet your mother in Florida? You know this aria very well, and I know you'll give a beautiful and heartfelt performance at the concert," said Maestro Fulgencio very confidently.

"I don't know what I'm going to do yet, but whatever I decide I will take some time to mourn properly. Thank you for calling, Maestro. I'll be in touch," said Sebastian.

Shortly afterward, Jonathan DiLorenzo called, but this time, Sebastian didn't pick up and let the answering machine answer the call. Jonathan answered the phone.

"Hi, Sebastian, it's me, Jonathan, I hope you're alright. I was very concerned about you at rehearsal today. Please call me when you can. Just want to make sure you're alright," said Jonathan.

At around 9 p.m., the phone rang again, and this time, it's Matthew Porter, the freelance journalist, who left a message earlier in the day to do a biography on Sebastian.

"Hello, Mr. Devereux. This is Matthew Porter, the freelance journalist. I know you're a busy man but would really love to write a biography on your life and would love to meet with you." At this point, Sebastian shook his head and then picked up the phone.

"Mr. Porter, I'm very sorry, but I really am not in the mood to do any lengthy interviews. I don't know if you're aware of this or not, but I just recently lost my grandmother and don't think I can take part in a biographical interview of my life at this time," replied Sebastian.

"Mr. Devereux, I am so sorry to hear about your grandmother. My deepest condolences to you and your family. But please, hear me out. I really would love to do this for my readers who are very interested in your career. I get letters from fans of yours who feel you have a great way of tapping into their emotions with your singing. I'll work around you and your schedule. We can approach it slowly if you like. Whenever you feel like stopping... we will stop. You are the boss! I will work around you."

"Mr. Porter, I am very flattered. Believe me, but I really don't think this is a very good idea," Replied Sebastian.

"Please, Mr. Devereux? I really want to do this for my readers. I promise I'll go at your pace," Pleaded Matthew.

"Alright, let me think about it, and I'll get back to you soon."

"Fair enough, Mr. Devereux. Have a good night," said Matthew.

At that moment, Sebastian felt quite torn in what was just proposed to him. Should Sebastian accept an interview with this freelance journalist whose work he had never heard of and trust him with his life story? Sebastian had every reason to be concerned and doubtful about divulging his personal life story to just any writer yet there was something about this freelance journalist that inspired a shred of confidence.

Still, Sebastian was intrigued with the idea of coming to terms with his past on his own terms. Nevertheless, Sebastian decided to read up on Matthew Porter's past work. He spent the next two hours reading some of Porter's published articles in some impressive journals, newspapers, and magazines. He had written a couple of biographies on three noteworthy musicians one of whom was a rock singer and the other was an easy-listening singer.

Sebastian could not find any written articles or biographies about any classical musicians or singers. This caused Sebastian to experience some trepidation about divulging his artistic life story to a writer who knew nothing about opera or his own career except for third-hand comments made by his fans. At that moment, Sebastian decided to call his good friend and colleague, Jonathan.

"Hello, Jonathan, It's Sebastian. I hope I didn't wake you but wanted to get back to you," said Sebastian.

"Sebastian! I am glad you called me back. Do not worry you didn't disturb me. How are you? I was very concerned when you left rehearsal so suddenly today. You seemed to be terribly upset, and I certainly can understand why," said Jonathan.

"Thank you, my dear friend. You are a true friend and scholar. I'm sorry about today, but I just felt so overwhelmed that I just couldn't continue singing the aria without breaking down and crying. After I left rehearsal, I drove off in my car and had a good cry and of course having a *tete-a-tete* with Mrs. Alba my housekeeper and you helped a great deal to put things into perspective for me," said Sebastian.

"I'm glad I could be of help, Sebastian, and I'll always be here for you. You and I go back a long way in our friendship, Seb. So, what did you do this evening?" asked Jonathan.

"It's funny you should ask. I just received a call this afternoon and this evening from a freelance writer who wants to interview me for a biography on my life. He sounded very persistent and determined to get me to agree to do this. I told him I would think about it after emphatically declining his offer. He says he would follow my lead and respect my boundaries. If that's true, then I guess I would have the upper hand and control the tone and content of the interview. That appeals to me. What do you think? Should I tell him I am interested and give him a chance?" asked Sebastian.

"Oh, yes! Absolutely you should give him a chance so long as you are in control of the conversation. Do not yield to anything that would go beyond your artistic boundaries. By the way, what is his name?" asked Jonathan.

"Exactly. His name is Matthew Porter. Have you heard of him?" asked Sebastian.

"Yes, I've heard of him, and he is excellent at his trade. Do it, Seb! I think you may very well need this to bring some closure and awakening to your life. When you open about yourself, it can, undoubtedly, be frightening, but I have complete faith you will blossom and be enriched by this kind of therapy as it were," said Jonathan.

"Well, after I hang up with you, I will call him back to tell him I will agree to meet with him. Thank you, dear friend. I will keep you informed. Have a good night," said Sebastian as he hung up the phone.

Shortly afterward Sebastian called back Matthew after he looked for his phone number which he left in the other room under some papers.

"Hello, is this Matthew Porter? This is Sebastian Devereux calling. In regard to your interview request, I have thought it over, and I will agree to meet with you. I would prefer we meet here at my place as I am not really up to meeting in a public venue at this time," said Sebastian.

"Mr. Devereux, I am glad you thought it over and reconsidered my offer. Certainly, I will be glad to meet you at your place. When would you like to meet? As I said before, I can work around your schedule as I am a freelance writer," Replied Matthew.

"Can you come on Monday for lunch at 12 p.m., and then we can talk, and if all goes well, we can get started right away?" asked Sebastian.

"That sounds fine to me," said Matthew delightedly. "My address is 1111 Cherry Pine Lane. I live in the Bayville condominium complex not far from the Bay Terrace shopping center. There is a doorman in the lobby who will have to call me on the intercom," said Sebastian.

"Don't worry. I will be there at 12 p.m. and look forward to meeting you," said Matthew.

"Well yes, that sounds good to me. Please do not be late," said Sebastian.

"Punctuality is my trademark. Don't worry. You won't regret this, Mr. Devereux," said Matthew.

"I'm counting on it. I will hopefully be able to come to terms on my terms. Good night, Mr. Porter," said Sebastian as he hung up with Matthew.

Chapter 2

It is now Monday morning, and Sebastian is getting ready to meet his potential biography writer with a sudden sense of trepidation which he tries to conceal with a forced sense of acting calmly. Sebastian chooses to wear a vertically striped green and white shirt from Tommy Hilfiger accompanied by a nicely fitting pair of tan chinos and brown penny loafers.

Sebastian is so nervous that he is trying to figure out how to comb his hair. He mulls over the body language of slicked-back versus parted on the side. Finally, he decides to go with the safe option of parted on the side to show he is conservative in his demeanor. Mrs. Alba suddenly arrives to prepare lunch for Sebastian and his guest Matthew Porter, the freelance writer.

"Good morning, Mrs. Alba. How are you this morning?" asked Sebastian.

"Good morning, Mr. Sebastian. I hope you had a good weekend. How is Mrs. Vanessa? When will she be returning from Florida?" asked Mrs. Alba.

"I spoke to Mom on Saturday night. She is having a fabulous time with my aunt Valeria. They went all over Sarasota, and when they got bored with soaking up culture at venues like the John Ringling museum and the outlet stores and UT mall, then they went cruising with mom's dear friend Alexis. Since Alexis has retired from working, she has really let her hair down and has truly become a lady of leisure. She swims in her pool and drinks peach margaritas until the sun comes up. Oh, maybe I'm exaggerating just a tad but not by much," said Sebastian slyly.

"Ohhhh, Mr. Sebastian, don't say that. Mrs. Alexis deserves to have this magic in her life now, And it is very good that Mrs. Vanessa and Mrs. Alexis are still such good friends and get together whenever your mother stays in Florida for the winter months," said Mrs. Alba.

"I suppose so. *Changing the subject* Mrs. Alba what are you preparing for lunch for my guest and me? What delectable delicacies will you grace our table with today?" asked Sebastian coyly.

"Well, I figure since you both will be working very hard on your interview for your book, I shouldn't make anything with too many carbs which will make you sleepy like tryptophan. So I decided to prepare a fillet mignon steak with sweet potato and green salad. I hope this will be satisfactory, Mr. Sebastian?" asked Mrs. Alba.

"Yes, that'll be fine, Mrs. Alba. I hope I'm not making a mistake in going through with this interview! I spoke to Jonathan last week, and he assured me I'd be in very good hands," said Sebastian cautiously.

"Mr. Sebastian, you are going through a lot of pain with the loss of your beloved grandmother, Mrs. Rita. She certainly loved you very much! I remember before she died, she shared with me how proud she was of you. She said you were a late bloomer who had to wait a long time for your big break but that you finally were rewarded with a beautiful singing career. I certainly agree with that!" said Mrs. Alba.

"Aww, thanks, Mrs. Alba. My grandmama actually said that? She would always tell me 'better late than never'. I guess that has been my motto in life. Everyone has always accomplished their dreams a wee faster than I. Just look at my cousins Leslie, Eddie, and Nick. Leslie married extremely well and now has a gorgeous home on the north shore of Long Island; Eddie has become a police captain; and Nick is a successful lawyer. Don't misunderstand me I'm very happy for all of them, and they deserve their happiness, but I just wish my success didn't take three decades to arrive," said Sebastian pensively.

"Well, Mr. Sebastian, I better get started with preparing the meal. Mr. Porter will be here soon. Lunch should be ready in 45 minutes," said Mrs. Alba.

In the meantime, as Mrs. Alba exited Sebastian's den to prepare lunch for Mr. Porter and him, Sebastian proudly looked at his very neatly stacked recital CD of his favorite opera singers as well as his favorite opera box sets. Five minutes later, the intercom bussed as the doorman announced Mr. Porter's arrival. Mrs. Alba asked him to send up Mr. Porter as he has been expected.

"Mr. Sebastian… Mr. Porter has arrived and is on his way up," said Mrs. Alba excitedly.

"Thank you, Mrs. Alba. I'm ready!" said Sebastian very determinedly.

25

Two minutes later, the doorbell rang, and as Mrs. Alba answered the door, she experienced a feeling of butterflies in her stomach anticipating the arrival of Mr. Porter an important new arrival in Mr. Sebastian's life.

"Good afternoon, Mr. Porter, I presume?" asked Mrs. Alba.

"Good afternoon, Mr. Devereux is expecting me. I'm Matthew Porter, a freelance writer and biographer," Responded Matthew with a slightly nervous chuckle.

"Yes. Mr. Sebastian is expecting you. Won't you come in?" asked Mrs. Alba.

Matthew entered and was very impressed by this spacious and brightly lit Hollywood-style apartment. The apartment was elegantly furnished and had a cherrywood baby grand piano at the entrance of the living room as one had to climb two steps upward to enter. It was elegantly decorated without being too pretentious. It had a warm and inviting feel to it. Mrs. Alba motioned for Mr. Porter to have a seat.

"Mr. Porter, please have a seat as Mr. Sebastian is in the den preparing for today's meeting with you, and he'll be out shortly to join you. Can I get you anything to drink meanwhile you wait for Mr. Sebastian?" asked Mrs. Alba.

"No, thank you. I'm fine. I'll wait until we are seated for lunch," said Mr. Porter.

As Mrs. Alba exited the living room, Mr. Porter took out his notebook and started looking all around to admire Sebastian's paintings and articles that adorned his apartment and began writing in his notebook. Five minutes later, Sebastian joins Mr. Porter in the living room.

"Ah, Mr. Porter, I presume. It's very nice to meet you at last. I'm Sebastian Devereux," said Sebastian politely but warmly.

"Wow! It's a great honor to meet my very first opera singer. Thank you for agreeing to meet with me, Mr. Devereux," said Mr. Porter warmly as he shakes Sebastian's hand with a polite but sincere grasp.

"I hope you didn't have any trouble finding the place? I know it can be a little tricky when you turn right onto my street and then have to make a sharp right toward my building. It is on a dead-end street and parking can be rather scarce in this neighborhood, to say the least," said Sebastian very concerned.

"Aw, don't worry; this meeting is very important to me and would have done whatever necessary to find your apartment even if I needed to ask for help from the National Guard!" said Mr. Porter jokingly.

"You're very kind, Mr. Porter. Lunch should be almost ready as Mrs. Alba becomes quite an artist when she cooks," said Sebastian with a great deal of pride.

Fifteen minutes later, Mrs. Alba called Mr. Porter and Sebastian for lunch and escorted them to a beautiful step-up dining room. Mrs. Alba escorted Mr. Porter to the table, and Sebastian decided to sit to the right of Mr. Porter so as to create a more inviting lunch experience as he started to feel comfortable communicating with Mr. Porter.

"Mr. Sebastian, I will now bring out the salad course. What would you both like to drink?" asked Mrs. Alba.

"I'll have a ginger ale," said Mr. Porter.

"I'll have the same," said Sebastian.

Mrs. Alba brought out the salad course followed by the main entrée which consisted of an 8-oz fillet mignon steak with baby potatoes and Brussels sprouts.

"How is the steak?" asked Sebastian.

"It's excellent! Mrs. Alba is an excellent cook. You are one lucky man, Mr. Devereux," said Mr. Porter.

"Thank you, Mr. Porter. Indeed, I am. Mrs. Alba has been like a caring aunt to me. Whenever I'm feeling down or excited, I turn to Mrs. Alba for her sage words of wisdom. I feel at home whenever she is around," said Sebastian calmly.

"Mr. Devereux, please call me Matthew. I would feel more at ease if you did. So, Mr. Devereux, what are you performing right now?" asked Matthew with keen interest.

"Well, Matthew, presently I am working on a benefit concert as one of a dozen soloists as the proceeds will go to benefit our favorite charities. They allow us to select two of our favorite arias. I have chosen *E La Solita Storia* by Cilea from the opera *L'Arlesiana* which sadly is never performed anymore. Matthew, the Opera world now is quite different from when Luciano Pavarotti performed in his glory days. Opera impresarios only want performers to sing roles that sell out theaters whether the roles are good for their voices or not. That is why I admire the artistry of Alfredo Kraus, Nicolai Gedda, and Fritz Wunderlich because these tenors would only sing operatic roles which were suitable for their voices. This is sorely lacking today. But I'll get more into that later. After all, we have a whole interview to discuss these wonderful topics!" exclaimed Sebastian with great conviction.

"Wow! My yes, I can already tell this interview is going to be quite stimulating as I love to interview artists who share their convictions about their art," said Matthew.

As they finished their main courses, Mrs. Alba cleared their main course and offered them dessert. She brought a lightly whipped strawberry and blueberry cheesecake with whipped cream with coffee for Matthew and a relaxing chamomile tea for Sebastian as it helped him to relax.

"Thank you, Mrs. Alba, that was sheer delight!" declared Matthew.

"I concur, Mrs. Alba. What would I do without you?" declared Sebastian rhetorically.

"Aww, thank you, Mr. Sebastian. I love working for this wonderful man and his wonderful mother," said Mrs. Alba as she looked at Matthew and smiled as she said it as if she were a proud mother doting on her talented son. But made no mistake. Mrs. Alba knew who was boss and only worked for Sebastian and his mother Vanessa in a supportive role. Sebastian and Matthew were both finishing up their dessert, but Sebastian asked about some of the people and topics Matthew had written about.

"So tell me, Matthew, who are some of the people and celebrities you have written about?" asked Sebastian coyly.

"Well, I have written about a few local politicians and some musicians but mostly rock bands and a few aspiring rock and pop singers but nobody nearly as famous as you," said Matthew protectively but warmly.

"Wow, anybody I know?" asked Sebastian flirtatiously.

"I doubt it. But now I know I will write about an artist with real artistic quality, and I'm sure has a great biography," said Matthew proudly.

"Wow… thank you for your kind words. Humbly speaking, I put all my heart and soul into everything I do whether it was my education, jobs I held as I was studying music, and now as a singer. Even trying to be the best son I can be to my mother I give it my all," said Sebastian gushingly.

"Well, I must say I certainly enjoyed this wonderful lunch Mrs. Alba has prepared for us. I am now eagerly awaiting our interview today. I am ready whenever you are," said Matthew.

Sebastian took a hint from Matthew as an hour had passed, and the clock was approaching 1 p.m., and it looked like both men were eager to begin their interview. Sebastian called for Mrs. Alba to come to the dining room. Mrs. Alba approached Sebastian.

"Mrs. Alba, thank you very much. Lunch was delicious! I think Mr. Porter and I are ready to begin our interview. We will probably be conducting the interview in the den in private," said Sebastian as if he were giving Mrs. Alba special instructions. Matthew echoed Sebastian's sentiment about the delicious lunch and smiled warmly.

"Yes, Mr. Sebastian. I'll be doing the laundry downstairs, and please text me if you need anything. Do you think you'll want me to prepare a light supper for you gentleman?" asked Mrs. Alba warmly.

"If we do, I'll let you know either by text or will call you via intercom. Everything depends on how far along we are in our interview," said Sebastian.

"Very good, Mr. Sebastian. It was a pleasure meeting you, and if there is anything you need, please let me know," said Mrs. Alba to Sebastian and Matthew.

Mrs. Alba exited the dining room as Sebastian and Matthew left the dining room and entered the den. Sebastian showed Matthew his CD collection very proudly, and Matthew looked with great admiration and took it all in with great and genuine interest. Shortly afterward, both men were seated, and Sebastian seemed a bit nervous but excited at the same time.

Mathew took out his writing pad and pens. He settled into the very comfortable leather chair but still was very much alert and ready to begin the interview.

"Well, Mr. Devereux. I just want to start by saying I am very much looking forward to this interview. I feel as if I am going to learn a great deal about you and the beautiful world of opera. But please understand, there is no specific order or sequence we need to follow. Begin where you want to begin. But if you want to start from your childhood and work your way toward adulthood that would also work well," said Matthew comfortingly.

"You don't want to hear anything about my childhood. It is boring and deranged!" said Sebastian jokingly.

"Now I'm even more intrigued!" said Matthew pressingly.

"Alright, you asked for it. So as my beautiful grandmama, Rita, used to say… strike while the iron is hot," said Sebastian resolutely.

Chapter 3

Sebastian now began to settle more comfortably into his leather beige chaise. He almost assumed the position of a patient in a therapy session only without the usual trappings of talking to a therapist with a small goatee and glasses who smoked a pipe. Sebastian's therapist was a biographer who struck an uncanny resemblance to an early 30ish Bradley Cooper who took out a pair of glasses and rested them on his forehead in a studious way.

"Well, Mr. Devereux. Are you ready to begin? Are you ready to take this journey that has now led you to your exciting and successful present? I just want you to know you are in charge, and your fans are looking forward to learning about the man behind the voice," said Matthew.

"Well, my name is Sebastian Devereux, and I just recently turned 41, on April 29 to be exact. I was born in Ridgewood Queens, as a matter of fact, half of my apartment was on the Brooklyn side, and the other half was on the Queens side. As a matter of fact, when I was four years old, I remember yelling across the avenue at my friends born on the Brooklyn side. My mom would come out and tell me to hush up as it wasn't very becoming of a child to be yelling across the street. My mom was very particular about behavior and maintaining good appearances," said Sebastian jokingly.

Both Sebastian and Matthew began to chuckle with light-hearted amusement at that moment.

"It sounds to me like your mother is a straight-laced caring woman," said Matthew.

"Yeah, my mom is a very special woman, and we have been through a lot together as you'll learn later on in our interview. All the women in my life have all been strong and formidable forces to be reckoned with each woman in her own way," said Sebastian proudly.

"Mr. Devereux, why don't you begin by describing your first and then some of your other childhood memories?" asked Matthew respectfully but boldly.

"Well, my very first memory as a child was at the age of two. I was in a warm climate being thrown up and down in very warm salty water. I remember my grandfather, Anibal, throwing me up and down in the water, and I being afraid of drowning but then shortly afterward gained a newly founded confidence realizing I'd be fine. I even remember tasting the saltwater in my fingers like it was a salty warm soup. I guess it was because we were in Caribbean waters. You see my mother was born in a city called Barranquilla spelled B A R R A N Q U I L L A. I want to make sure you spell that correctly," said Sebastian.

"Got it! Please continue," said Matthew.

"Well, we were visiting my mother's family in Colombia. My mother was already married to my father

James who at that time was a law student and had the summer off from school. My maternal grandparents Gabriela and Anibal wanted my mother, father, and I to join them in visiting Colombia after so many years of them being away.

"My father James as I was told was quite reluctant about it at first and declined their offer, but my grandfather, Anibal, had a way of convincing my father and got him to see it his way. So, then we were off to Colombia, and from what I heard, it wasn't exactly an uneventful vacation as my mother became ill in a city called Cali spelled C A L I. Just think of a shortened California spelling.

"She developed blisters all over her body and the doctor advised her to travel to the Caribbean coast to bathe in the warm salty water. So my grandparents decided we'd all go to Santa Marta, and they have a beautiful beach called El Rodadero, which is a backdrop of the Sierra Nevada de Santa Marta. It is said that a person could ski on that mountain during the day and then bathe in the warm waters of the beach in the late afternoon. It enjoys the best of both worlds. Thankfully, my mom fully recovered, and we returned home to the U.S.A. after three weeks of being in Colombia," said Sebastian with great relief.

"Wow! That must have been quite an adventure for all of you!" exclaimed Matthew.

"Yes, it was. Yet, I have never returned to Colombia after that time. I have friends who would love for me to visit, but for some reason, it doesn't seem like a thing for me to do right now in my life. I just want to be close to home. Thankfully, I have traveled to Europe when I sang in Naples, Hamburg, London, and Vienna. I'm certainly glad

I did it when I did it, but now, I just wish to remain in the United States," said Sebastian pensively.

"Yes. So, going back to your childhood, what other childhood memories do you recall?" asked Matthew gently but pressingly.

"Well, I was very much a schemer. I had a childhood neighbor named Gianni who was about three months younger, and he was always indoors. His mother was very protective of him and wouldn't let him go outside without her or his father. I used to talk to him when I was outside on my stoop, and he would talk to me from his bedroom window.

"I remember asking him to come out and play with me, but Gianni said he wasn't allowed outside without his parents. I remember feeling so sorry for him that one day, I had a red toy swivel chair that I took out outside with me. My mother asked where I was going with it, but I simply replied that I was going outside with to sit and talk to my friend from our stoop. Naturally, my mom believed me. I mean what good mother could ever doubt her own angelic-faced son?" said Sebastian with a tongue-in-cheek look.

Matthew laughed heartily at that statement but was taking notes feverishly but smilingly at the same time as if he thought he had Pulitzer- prized material in his possession.

"Anyway, my mom was putting rollers in her hair and warned me not to go beyond our stoop as she didn't want me to go too far away as we were getting ready to go and visit my grandparents, Rita and Poppy Rocco. I agreed to my mother's request, but then when I got outside, I saw poor Gianni staring outside from his window. I remember telling Gianni that he should come over and play with me, but he said he wasn't allowed outside.

"Not giving up I invited Gianni over for ice cream, and he'd still have enough time to sneak back into his room if he did. I taking charge at that moment ordered my sheltered friend to put on his sneakers so he could come outside. The poor kid had unmatched shoes thrown all over the place, and he put on a mismatched pair of sneakers after five minutes of looking at shoes literally flying across the room.

"So as not to lose more time, I told him that would be fine and to climb out of his window. But he said the window sill was too high even from his street-level window. I placed my red tow swivel chair under his window sill and ordered him to step down onto it. Gianni did climb down with my help and we both jumped for joy triumphantly but then hushed up so as not to alert his mother to our cries of jubilation for his temporary escape from home.

"I took Gianni's hand, and we marched toward our delicious prize waiting for us. My mother answered the door and was shocked at what she saw! I remember her saying, 'Seby, what are you both doing here! How did you get your friend Gianni to get permission to leave his home?' Well, I took my red swivel chair and put it underneath his window, helped him pick out sneakers so he could come outside, and now we are here for our delicious ice cream," said Sebastian confidently yet angelically.

"Sweetheart, Gianni is wearing two different sneakers... he looks like a clown! What are we going to tell his mother when she discovers he is missing?" exclaimed Vanessa.

"Oh, Mommy, we'll have our ice cream, and then I'll sneak Gianni right back through his bedroom window and his mom won't know anything," said Sebastian.

"Seby! Okay, come on boys. I'll serve you a small dish of ice cream as we have to go out. Your grandparents are waiting for us. We're expected for dinner and you know how your grandmother wants us to come with good appetites," said Vanessa.

"Okay, Mommy. Yey! We're gonna have ice cream!" exclaimed Sebastian.

Sebastian and Gianni were like kids in a candy store after his mom, Vanessa, served them what look like two small hot fudge sundaes. They lapped it up like the most delicious dessert both boys had ever eaten. Then Sebastian further recalls how they took Gianni home to explain what happened to his mother.

"I remember my mom telling us that we were to finish our ice cream, and then as soon as she finishes dressing, we'd take Gianni home the right way and not sneakily like the way he came over to our apartment. I remember we knocked on the door, and Gianni's mom, Mrs. Gambini, answered and could not believe what she had seen. She was initially very upset, but then she met my mother and calmed down as she realized I just wanted to invite him over for ice cream.

"As a matter of fact, both of our mothers became good friends from that day on, and Mrs. Gambini didn't mind her

Gianni hanging out with me and having ice cream together once in a while. I attribute this to my mother's honesty, and Mrs. Gambini appreciated that. I admire my mother's integrity, and to this day, I will always be grateful that she always wanted to do things the correct way as she described it. She is my rock after The Lord of course," said Sebastian proudly.

"Wow, you were a bit devilish from what I hear from you," said Matthew.

"Well, I would say more angelic than devilish but if I had to equate it I'd say 80%/20% angelic/devilish. Ha. Humbly speaking, I'd say I was a good boy with occasional no infrequent devilish tendencies. But whatever I did I always did it with the intention to do good for others," said Sebastian.

"In other words, are you saying the ends justify the means?" asked Matthew probingly.

"I suppose so. Yes, sometimes one must resort to unconventional means to do good so long as it is nothing criminal or hurtful toward others. I mean I like to think we helped Gianni to face his fears and step out of his comfort zone that day and thanks to my mother we were able to help Gianni and his mother as she learned that day she could trust someone else who was responsible to own up to what had happened that day. I will always thank my mother for that.

"As it turned out Gianni and I would hang out together for a while after that time he came over to my apartment for ice cream. My mother would take us to the neighborhood park and a few times for pizza on Myrtle Avenue. We were even in the same kindergarten class for a year, but then my parents and grandparents decided they wanted us all to live in a more residential area, so we moved to Bayside, Queens.

"My grandparents sold their beautiful English Tudor in Hollis Hills. From what my mother described she said it was huge. It had four bedrooms a huge staircase leading up to the bedrooms and had a sunken living room and a step-up dining room adorned with beautiful paintings, a china closet, and a dining room table, which seated 8–10 people," said Sebastian.

"Wow, it sounds like your grandparents were quite wealthy! What did your grandfather do for a living?" exclaimed Matthew.

"Well, from what I know he was a real estate broker and owned his own firm. My grandmother Rita at this point in her life was a lady of leisure. Anyway, they sold their home, and my father, James, was already preparing to take the bar exam and wanted us to live in a better neighborhood. So when I was five years old my parents turned over the apartment to the landlady, and we then moved to Bayside, and my grandparents bought a beautiful Victorian-style home.

"I remember it was December 1, and we moved to that house a week before my grandparents, and we got everything ready for their arrival. I remember it was a brisk and very cold Saturday morning, and I had to say goodbye to my friend Gianni. I remember wearing a horizontally striped green, yellow, and brown shirt with green pants, and my hair was long as I needed a haircut, but with all of the commotion of moving, my mother couldn't take me for a haircut.

"I went up to Gianni with my red swivel chair only this time I stood on it and reached for Gianni to give him a hug. I told him I'd write to him, but of course, that never happened. Mrs. Gambini came to the window, and she wished me and my family well and as my mom came to get me. Both ladies shook each other's hands and said their goodbyes. My father had no interest in saying goodbye to anyone as he was eager to leave this neighborhood.

"My father, James, yelled 'Let's go Vanessa and Seb! It's time to embrace our future'. At age 5, I didn't understand anything he said, but I figured as long as I was with my parents I'd be in very good hands," said Sebastian.

"Wow. So what other stories do you recall from your childhood?" asked Matthew.

"Well, I didn't have many friends as a child. I remember when we used to visit my other grandmother Gabriela's house in Ozone Park, and I used to run around with my younger cousin Eddie. I would always run while looking backward. It was the strangest habit I had! My aunt Valeria used to worry about me so much. She would say 'Seby, be careful, honey, you could fall and get hurt!' But then my uncle Roberto would assure my aunt not to worry about me as I was a kid and needed to be free to run and play.

"My cousin Eddie and I would run all around the outside of the house. My cousin Eddie was three years younger than me and he would always want whatever I had. I remember I had a beautiful yellow and blue tricycle which I truly loved, but he always wanted it and he used to take it without asking. He saw it as his for the taking, not for the asking. We would get into arguments and even a few punching and shoving matches. I can't believe that I recall

41

all of this, but it all starts coming back to me," said Sebastian.

"Well, that's to be expected. Personally, I am learning a great deal about you and your early childhood. I can't wait to see where this goes next!" said Matthew.

"Well, Eddie and I had what I would call now a love-hate relationship. I would say we were never close but merely tolerated each other because we were so different. It was a lot easier for me to love our cousin, Leslie. She and I were the first grandchildren to be born on my mother's side of the family. Leslie was my aunt Maria and my uncle Stachu's daughter. He adored her and in his eyes, she could do no wrong. They had a nice home in Bayside not far from where we lived, but she attended a different school at that time.

"Leslie was more like a sister than a cousin, and Eddie and I used to fight over her for her attention. Leslie loved both of us, but she would always admit to me that I was her favorite cousin so I didn't mind keeping her secret," said Sebastian with a smile on his face.

"I remember my cousin, and I used to play tricks on people like my grandmother, Gabriela, like when we would use her bed as a trampoline only to end up causing the box spring to come loose. We would call my aunt Valeria and mother to come to survey the damage.

"My aunt Valeria was a good but nervous woman, and she would come in like a Sargent and would fix the box spring with my mother. She would say 'Oh, my God! Could you imagine if our parents were to lie down? They would come flying down and crashing through my ceiling!' I had to prevent myself from laughing and peeing on myself.

They would go to work on fixing the box spring and crossed their fingers hoping everything would be fine.

"I remember another time Eddie and I would play tricks on my grandmother like pushing my grandmother Gabriela into a small storage closet. Thankfully, we let her out of it after five seconds. She was angry and rightly so, but she never tattled on us to our mothers. At first, I thought she was too strict, but then in time, I came to understand her emotionally, and once I learned to speak Spanish, we had a lot of nice conversations. She was a remarkable woman in her own right but more about that later.

"I also remember a time when I was going on vacation with my parents, and my mother told me I went up to this woman seated by her husband, and out of the blue, I caressed her calves. My mother ran over to me and pulled me away and apologized profusely to the lady and her husband. They were Texans, and the wife said, 'Oh sugar, don't worry. He's behaving like a nice curious little boy. Don't stifle him. It's good for him'," said Sebastian.

Sebastian and Matthew both laughed heartily at that moment, and one could see both men were now more comfortable in this interview than when they first started. Sebastian felt genuinely comfortable that he was getting in touch with his feelings and doing it on his own terms.

"In a nutshell, I'd say I got into some mischief when I was a little boy, but as time went on, I became more introverted and steered away from trouble to the best of my ability. I think it was probably due to life's cares as I will further explain later," said Sebastian.

"I'm certainly looking forward to discovering how this whole story unfolds," said Matthew.

Chapter 4

"So, Mr. Devereux, you have described some of your very early childhood experiences and some of the shenanigans you engaged in up until now. Care to share any other things you can remember? And please feel free to go beyond such as your primary years in school," said Matthew.

"Well, apart from spending time with my cousins Leslie and Eddie I basically had very few friends, but music and my family were a big part of my life," said Sebastian.

"Would you care to elaborate on that?" asked Matthew.

"Well, as a child, I used to love and gravitate toward television commercials and would even recite them from memory along with hand gestures and tone of voice. I especially would love to watch the movie bumpers. Do you know what those are? I think they would be a bit before your time. In the pre-cable days, we only had network channels which gave movies, kid shows, and news editorials. My favorite ones were WPIX 11, WORTV 9, and ABC 7. I remember anytime my mom had the living room television on I would immediately run out from my bedroom to watch the WORTV 9 bumper followed by the news editorial which would broadcast contrasting views on a given topic.

"I also loved to watch the WPIX 11 news and movie bumpers as they called them in those days. If you check out YouTube, they have some of those that were uploaded by fellow nostalgists like myself. I can't explain why I liked them so much, but I felt at the time those music bumpers resonated with something creative in me.

"Now as an adult they cause me to wax nostalgic. They were reminiscent of a time in my life when life was simpler and the great challenges coming my way were still a galaxy away. I also used to love to watch Vice President Richard M Hughes' Christmas message editorial from 1979 to 1984. It really resonated with the importance of Christ's birth and his beautiful example to all. Even as a child, I loved the things of Christ, and it would later serve to help me discover a new relationship with Him," said Sebastian.

"No, I can't say I have ever seen any of those TV bumpers, but I will now do my homework and research some of those. But they certainly sound fascinating. You certainly were pretty grown up for that age as most 4- and 5-year-old kids wouldn't be interested in TV bumpers as they would be more interested in playing with robots, action figures, and t-ball," said Matthew.

"Yes, I know. I think it served as a catalyst or a forerunner for my love of music and singing. I had absolutely no interest in playing sports as a child, but then later, I did acquire a taste for swimming and rowing. When I was in college, I joined a rowing team. As a child, I always loved bike riding. I think it was because it was an individual activity. Once we moved out of Ridgewood, we moved to Bayside to be closer to my paternal grandparents, Rita and Poppy Rocco," said Sebastian.

"Why don't you tell me about what life was like living with your grandparents and parents?" Asked Matthew.

"Well, we moved to Bayside Hills when I was five and a half years old. It was a beautiful residential neighborhood as I recall. It had a huge backyard, and it had a nice swing on the tree and my parents and grandparents decided to have a big pool put in the yard so as to be able to refresh ourselves during the summer, and I even had a few friends over to the house from time to time. I always remember there being a lot of barbecues, laughter, and special events such as my first Holy Communion, wedding anniversaries, and birthday parties. My grandparents always wanted there to be celebrations because life was all about being together and making the best of life," said Sebastian.

"Your grandparents sound like they were festive people who made most of life in every way," said Matthew.

"Well, my grandfather, Poppy Rocco as he was lovingly called, was a huge proponent of laughter and not taking life too seriously. I guess he figured the rest of the family was too intense already he figured he'd lighten the mood whenever possible. My father was very good at doing imitations of people he would come in contact with in graduate law school and now at his new law agency that Friday and Saturday evenings would be devoted to mini barbecue and potato chip and pretzel chip parties, and my father would make gin and tonics for all the adults and my grandfather, Poppy Rocco, was floating on Cloud nine. But as much fun and laughter as there was during those early years there was also moments of great stress," Warned Sebastian.

"In what way was there great stress, Mr. Devereux?" asked Matthew emphatically.

"Well, when I was being placed in kindergarten, my former kindergarten teacher strongly recommended to my parents that I attend a special education school because she was concerned, I was a very slow learner and emotionally immature compared with other children of my age. As a matter of fact, I attended preschool with my cousin Leslie. Our mothers thought it would be good for us to be in the same class together, but I was quite energetic and immature that it infuriated our preschool teacher, Miss Peggy. She was a stern-faced woman with short red hair. she looked like Mike's diabolical mother from the show Mike and Molly. She had her favorite students, and my cousin Leslie was one of them. I was bad at following directions and wanted to do things my way or as I saw it my own unique way.

"Whenever Miss Peggy saw my mother coming, she would always call my mother over to complain about me having to be in the corner and the fact I would never amount to anything worthwhile. My mother was indignant when she heard this and decided to not renew my registration for the spring semester and placed me in another kindergarten school. I think Miss Peggy was ecstatic when she learned I would not be returning for the following semester," said Sebastian.

"It sounds to me like your mother has always had your best interest at heart. Where was your father when all of this was happening?" asked Matthew.

"Well, my father was already working very hard to expand his law practice so he was constantly working and never had too much time for anything except what was strictly necessary concerning Mom and me. They did meet with the special education teacher. I was sent to for six months. I had to take a school van there, and when we discovered that they were giving students Ritalin to calm them, my parents and grandparents were outraged and demanded I be removed from that school immediately!

"The four of them had a family conference one evening and decided to confront the teacher, Mr. Ferraro, and demand I be removed from the clutches of this 'so-called' special educator Mr. Ferraro pleaded with my family not to make the mistake of doubting and questioning his credentials in diagnosing mentally challenged children as he called me. My parents and grandparents were adamant about pulling me out and enrolling me in a private Catholic school to help me. That fall, I was enrolled in St. Robert's school. My first few years were easy for me, but fortunately, I had the support of my family to help get me through the pain of adjusting to a new school," said Sebastian.

"Well, I'm glad to hear your family has been a supportive force in your life," said Matthew.

At this point, Matthew asked Sebastian if he would like to take a creative break to not have the interview go stale. Sebastian agreed and asked if he would like to have a light supper before they resume.

"Matthew why don't we take a break for a little while and then resume after a light supper?" asked Sebastian.

"Well, it is now 5:30. I wouldn't mind adjourning for a little while. I wouldn't mind eating something light while we work and talk," said Matthew.

49

"I'll ask Mrs. Alba to prepare us some finger sandwiches while I show you some of my CD and opera box set collection." Sebastian called Mrs. Alba from his cell phone. "Mrs. Alba, please prepare us some light finger sandwiches as Mr. Porter and I are going to work a little while longer," Asked Sebastian and then hung up.

"Matthew, come and take a look at my music collection while we wait for Mrs. Alba to bring us some finger sandwiches," said Sebastian.

Matthew got up from his comfortable chair to eagerly look at Sebastian's collection of opera box sets and individual singers. He looked with complete amazement as he had never seen such an immense wall of great artistry.

"Do you see this section? This is my soprano section individual arias and duets, and here to the right is my baritone and tenor section. I have an affinity for sopranos such as Maria Callas, Renata Tebaldi, Victoria de los Angeles, Anna Moffo, Montserrat Caballe, Leontyne Price, Martina Arroyo, and others... as for baritones, I enjoy the voices of Robert Merrill and Ettore Bastianini. As for tenors, I love Jussi Björling, Giuseppe Di Stefano, Carlo Bergonzi, Nicolai Gedda, Alfredo Kraus, and Jaime Aragall, he was a very nervous singer just like Franco Corelli, but when both men went out on stage to perform, they were superb! Corelli was so nervous before going on stage that his wife would have to yell out to him to have courage *Coraggio amore mio!*

"It is never easy to go out on stage, but you get used to it. But stage fright never goes away completely, you just learn to control it," said Sebastian.

"I never knew Franco Corelli battled with great stage fright during his career. I know of him because my grandmother had a couple of his CDs. She said he was famous for singing Calaf from *Turandot*," said Matthew happily as if he knew something he could bring to the table.

"Oh, yes, and he was dynamic as a singer and performer! When Franco Corelli entered a room or stepped onstage, he was charismatic. He had the voice of a burnished organ and the handsome virile look of a Hollywood movie star. He was also tall, and at the time when most tenors averaged between 5'6" and 5'8" tall, Mr. Corelli stood at a very impressive 6'1" tall. Mario Del Monaco also had similarities to Franco Corelli, and they sang similar roles, but I tend to be partial to Corelli. Yet, as much as I love all of these great singers, I always return to listening to the recordings of early José Carreras. I'll explain more about this when we meet again," said Sebastian.

"Well, Mr. Devereux, I think I have enough to work with from this session but would very much love to continue with part two of this interview. How would tomorrow work for you about 2 p.m.? Are you available?" asked Matthew eagerly.

"Yes, I think 2 p.m. would be fine. How many sessions do you anticipate it would take to complete this interview? My mother will be returning from Florida this Saturday and would really like to have it wrapped up by then," Asked Sebastian.

"Well, that depends on you. I would like to pick up where we left off tomorrow and then meet again for a third session to discuss your early opera chorus years to your eventual ascent to singing principal roles in New York and throughout Europe. If we need to do a 4th session, we could both decide how we would approach it. We can play it by ear," said Matthew.

"Well, I think that would be fine. I'd rather take it in stride than overwork ourselves to the point of exhaustion. I have the remainder of this week available as I'm on temporary leave because I am mourning for my grandmother who died a month ago," said Sebastian melancholically.

"I am very sorry, Mr. Devereux. We can take it slowly if a topic becomes too difficult for you to talk about during our upcoming interview sessions," said Matthew reassuringly.

"Thank you, Matthew. That is very reassuring and considerate of you. Are you sure you're not a psychologist? I feel as if I've been talking to a therapist today," said Sebastian jokingly.

"No, not really although I did take some psychology classes when I attended NYU. I feel a writer should be empathetic when he or she is interviewing people especially when they are doing biography writing for artists and celebrities such as yourself," said Matthew smilingly.

"Ah, I see, well that is gratifying and refreshing. I hope you don't mind if I put on music during our interview sessions together? It helps me to be more creative, but I figured I'd ask before doing so?" asked Sebastian.

"Oh, no, not at all. It also would give me more insight into what music motivates you. Would you also be playing any of your own recital or opera recordings?" asked Matthew excitedly.

"Oh, no! I never listen to my own recordings. It would simply drive me crazy as I tend to be very self-critical and perfectionistic. I enjoy listening to the recordings of all the great singers of the past as they have helped to mold me into the singer I've become today for better or worse," said Sebastian chucklingly.

"Oh, come now, Mr. Devereux! But I understand your feelings on the subject. Well, Mr. Devereux. It is almost 7:30, and I think it would be a very good idea to end our first session now and let's continue tomorrow. What time would be convenient for you? Remember, I will work around your schedule," said Matthew.

"How about we meet at 1 p.m.? We'll get started with the interview right away," said Sebastian to hintingly suggest there would be no introductory lunch this time.

"That'll be perfect, Mr. Devereux. Thank you for a delicious lunch and a very thorough and productive first meeting."

"You're welcome and thank you for so far making this a pleasant interview experience. Until tomorrow then," said Sebastian.

Both Sebastian and Matthew shook hands and wished each other a good night. Sebastian closed the door and thanked Mrs. Alba for her cooperation and for preparing a wonderful lunch for him and his guest. Mrs. Alba said her good night and met her husband downstairs ready to be picked up.

Sebastian calls his good friend Jonathan to let him know how his first interview session turned out.

"Hello, Jonathan? It's Seb. How are you my friend?" asked Sebastian nervously.

"Hi, Seb. I'm fine thanks. How was your first interview session with Matthew Porter?" asked Jonathan Porter curiously.

"Well, we had a delicious lunch at 12 p.m., thanks to Mrs. Alba, and then we got started after he asked me some questions about my art and music projects. Then he proceeded to ask about my early childhood experiences. It felt more like therapy. Ha ha," said Sebastian jokingly.

"Well, that's understandable. He wants to get as much biographical information on you as possible to make it a truly great biography. This is part of his job and I'm sure he does it very well," said Jonathan confidently.

"Yes, I suppose so. I just hope he doesn't cross any boundaries. After all, I have just lost my grandmother recently," said Sebastian nervously.

"Oh, don't worry Seb, just be yourself. You're an all-around great guy and will shine in this interviewer. Remember you don't have to answer any questions or touch any topics you don't want to. Being the professional Matthew Porter is I'm sure he'll know how to work around that to bring out the best in you to make your life story appeal to many readers. Have a good night my dear friend," said Jonathan reassuringly as he hung up with Sebastian.

Chapter 5

It was the following day, and Mathew arrived at Sebastian's apartment at 1 o'clock as promised and was sent up by the doorman. Mrs. Alba answered the door and welcomed Matthew to enter and wait for Sebastian to meet him for their next interview session.

"Mr. Porter, would you care for anything to drink?" asked Mrs. Alba.

"Yes, I'd love a glass of ginger ale if you have any," Replied Matthew.

"Very good sir, I'll be out with your ginger ale momentarily," said Mrs. Alba.

Five minutes later, Sebastian emerged from his den and cordially greeted Matthew followed by Mrs. Alba bringing out Matthew's requested glass of ginger ale.

"Hello, Matthew, I hope I haven't kept you waiting too long?" asked Sebastian as he shook Matthew's hand.

"No, not at all, Mr. Devereux. I was just mentally preparing for our meeting today," Replied Matthew.

"Here is your ginger ale, Mr. Porter," said Mrs. Alba as she gently handed the glass of ginger ale to Matthew, and he thanked her with a smile.

"Mrs. Alba no calls today as I will be working with Mr. Porter in my den all afternoon," said Sebastian.

"Yes sir. Would you both like a snack while you're working? Perhaps around 5 p.m.?" asked Mrs. Alba.

"Yes, that'll be fine Mrs. Alba," said Sebastian while he motioned Matthew to enter his den.

"Please be seated, Matthew. Yesterday was quite an introductory session. I'm surprised you came back," said Sebastian jokingly.

"For me, it was a pleasure, Mr. Devereux. I can see there is more than meets the eye in interviewing you," said Matthew.

At that moment, both men chuckled, and Sebastian settled into his comfortable leather recliner while Matthew took out his pen and notebook to write with great fervor.

"So, Mr. Devereux, I have learned quite a bit about your early childhood and parents and grandparents. Tell me more about them. How did your parents and grandparents meet?" asked Matthew.

"Well, I'll start with my paternal grandparents. My grandmother was named Rita by her mother Margie, short for Marguerite. My grandmama says she named her Rita because she liked Rita Hayworth and thought she looked like her. My grandmama was a very beautiful woman. She had reddish-brown hair almost like an auburn red. She was born on 3 June 1926, and her mother Margie was French-

Irish and born on 7 February 1906, and her father, Yener, was born on 12 April 1896, in Ankara, Turkey but raised in Istanbul. He was exactly ten years her senior. My grandmother says she was born on Middleton Street in Williamsburg, Brooklyn.

"She says her mother told her there was a huge rainstorm on the day she was born. She told me she and her family were always moving every couple of months like gypsies. She never could grow comfortable living anywhere for too long which we think may be why my poor grandfather had to constantly buy and sell their condos and homes because my grandmother would grow bored living in any one place for too long.

"My grandmother was a wonderful storyteller, and we would get together on Friday and Saturday nights, and she would often share some of her childhood stories with us. I remember one Saturday night I asked Grandmama to tell us about her early childhood. Grandmama gladly accepted the request and often told us how much she hated school as a child.

"She said she had a second-grade teacher named Miss Coombs, and she one day was telling a story to the class seated on a high stool and recalled that she desperately needed to use the bathroom or washroom as they called it. When suddenly Grandmama raised her hand, Miss Coombs abruptly motioned for her to put her down as she did not want to be disturbed during story time. My poor grandmother was very antsy and yelled out that she needed to use the restroom, but Miss Coombs refused to listen when suddenly Grandmama soiled herself in public and all the kids mockingly pointed at Grandmama as the guilty culprit who caused this foul stench to infest class 2-B.

"You can imagine how mortified my grandmother was and she ran out of the classroom sobbingly. Her beautiful white stockings and pink dress were completely soiled, and two boys were yelling mockingly at her. Mrs. Coombs finally realized what she had done too little too late and sent Grandmama home to be cleaned and changed.

"My great grandmother saw my grandmama was completely soiled and red with humiliation but still insisted she had to go back to school lest she never returned to school ever again. She cleaned her completely and marched with my grandmother back to school to confront Miss. Coombs. Great grandma was quite eccentric, to say the least. She yelled at Mrs. Coombs for allowing her poor Rita to be utterly humiliated publicly. Grandmama says Mrs. Coombs tried to justify her actions only to be met with a very unexpected backlash. She told Mrs. Coombs she hoped she would go to a dance one night and soil herself in front of hundreds of people on the dance floor!" said Sebastian laughingly.

"Oh, my goodness! Wow! I certainly didn't expect your great grandmother to say that to her!" said Matthew laughing hysterically.

"Trust me, neither did Miss Coombs, the school principal, vice principal, the other teachers, or Grandmama's classmates! But something good came of it as Miss Coombs told my grandmama that whenever she needed to go to the washroom to just take the block pass and go!

"Another event happened when my grandmama was a little girl when a Jewish woman took a brick and hit Grandmama on the head simply because she loitered on her property. The lady took great grandma to court and there was a lot of name-calling, but my great grandmother and grandmama won their case and the other woman was ordered to pay small monetary damages and not to go near them again! Great grandma also pushed the woman against the wall and threatened her to never ever hurt her Rita again!

"Grandmama also had a younger sister named Millie who was two years her junior, but they had very different personalities and really went their separate ways as adults. Grandmama admitted to me that they never offered her help even to help take care of Great Grandma Margie when she lived with Grandmama and my father, James, and Aunt Shirley.

"My grandmother admitted she was spoiled as a little girl as she always received the attention and adulation and was even awarded the better doll of the two. Grandmama received Mary Jane; a very beautiful doll while Aunt Millie was given a smaller doll named Blue Bell," said Sebastian analytically.

At this point, Matthew was not about to break Sebastian's momentum as he knew he was building up to something important.

"My grandmama grew up but sadly quit school when she was only 14 years old. I often lamented over this decision she made as I firmly believe Grandmama could have made a great detective, judge, or interior decorator if she had applied herself. She met a man named James Devereux, and after a short while, she married him. He was a truck driver, and she liked but never loved him. He was a wanderer, and he would leave my grandmother for weeks on end and only return for a very short time. They lived in a cold-water shack in Connecticut. They were forced to live with his sister Rosie, but she was not very empathetic to my grandmama's plight.

"Once, my grandmother was pregnant with my aunt Shirley and later my father, her money was scarce and Grandmama was frightened that she was alone and wouldn't have enough money to take care of herself or her small children. My grandmama called for help from her mother and sister, but neither one could offer her any financial assistance, so she knew she had to get away with her kids. Strangely, Rosie offered Grandmama some help but warned her not to tell James Sr. as she could get in trouble with him. My grandmama was just grateful for the help that she gladly kept her part of the bargain.

"My grandmama was a proud woman and would never take public assistance as she had to go out and find jobs working in factories. She raised my Aunt Shirley, whom she named after Shirley Jones as she struck a remarkable resemblance to her and my father, James Jr., as my great grandmother loved James Cagney and, therefore, wanted him to be named after him.

"Life was not easy for my grandmama, Rita, as she had two kids with very distinct personalities. Aunt Shirley was more dutiful, loving, and friendly and was, therefore, better able to get along with my grandmama. My father on the other hand was very spoiled, demanding, and jealous and was of the notion that life revolved around him according to my grandmama and others in the family.

"Yet, I once spoke with my second cousin Deborah who was pretty and outgoing and very similar to Grandmama as people thought she should have been her daughter. She believed that Grandmama and Aunt Shirley left my father out of events, but I think it was because he was so spoiled that he made it difficult for them to get along with him. Cousin Deborah loved both cousins, but she saw both sides of the story and said things weren't as black and white as you might think. Cousin Deborah went to college, at my grandmama's insistence and became a handwriting analyst for the F.B.I.

"Grandmama was so impressed with her penmanship that she strongly encouraged her to pursue that dream… and she did and hasn't looked back since! We talk every now and then, but I am very happy for her success," said Sebastian.

"Wow! I really am learning a great deal about your grandmother and great-grandmother. They were very strong-willed women, but it sounds like it served them well. So, what about your grandfather, Poppy Rocco?" said Matthew.

"Well, I don't know very much about his past as he was a secretive but very good man! I know he was born on the other side of the Brooklyn Queens Expressway in Williamsburg on the Italian side. He admitted they were very poor also but didn't seem to have the family drama my grandmother had with her parents.

"Grandmama's father, Yener, used to cheat on Great Grandma Margie, and would wash the backs of the young women who lived in their flat. She knew of this but never did anything about it. Getting back to Poppy Rocco. His father became big in local politics as he became the general superintendent of Sanitation and then they became more comfortable financially. They became proprietors of the Italian meat markets called Calabrese Italian products.

"The only thing I can tell you about his childhood was that he and his neighborhood friends had a naughty habit of pulling the fire alarms on the street corners and run away with his friends to escape punishment by the police. His poor mother, Nettie, would have to stop talking to her next-door neighbors to help get Poppy Rocco to safety. She was never mad at him though as she adored him, and he could do no wrong in her eyes," said Sebastian laughingly.

"As for how they met? Well, it was late 1966 and Grandmama one day went into one of the Calabrese meat markets as luck would have it and she met a man named Carlo who was talking and laughing with Grandmama Rita. He liked her, but of course, Grandmama wasn't attracted to him as she just liked talking to him. He asked her out on a date on Saturday night and she accepted capriciously but not expecting anything serious to happen. He took my grandmama's phone number to confirm for Saturday night.

"The funniest thing happened though as she did get a call on Friday night, it was not from Carlo but from Rocco, his cousin. My grandmama couldn't believe it was another man calling and was wondering what this was all about. He said Carlo couldn't make it on Saturday night but wanted to take her out in his place. At first, she was a bit reluctant, but then she thought to herself why not take a chance.

"Grandmama agreed and met him by the Williamsburg Saving Bank in downtown Brooklyn which was a very busy thoroughfare and could not park around there. The idea was to pick up my grandmama and drive off in the car together. She saw him and didn't think she liked him from first glance as he was unshaven. She was, therefore, mulling the idea of turning away, but he opened the passenger side window and advised her to either get in or not as he had to drive away due to heavy traffic behind him.

"Grandmama was truly at a crossroads in her life as she wasn't sure what to do. Poppy Rocco assured her she'd be safe and if she wanted to get off at the next block, she was free to do so and that would be the end of it. Grandmama decided to throw caution to the wind and go out with Poppy Rocco.

"After being in the fight or flight position next to the passenger door she relaxed, and they went to a bar and grill for a drink and barbecued ribs. They laughed and talked for almost three hours and they decided to go out on another date only the next time it was to a very fancy Chinese restaurant and Poppy Rocco was neatly dressed in one of his signature suits and was clean-shaven. But before they started seriously dating there was a period of about a month when Grandmama Rita hadn't heard from Poppy Rocco and the famous Vikki Carr song *It Must Be Him* was playing on the radio and she wanted him to call, but he hadn't called. Once Poppy Rocco and Grandmama Rita dated for almost six months, she decided to become Rita Calabrese," said Sebastian.

63

"Wow, so that is a brief history of your paternal grandparents! Did you ever meet your blood-related grandfather, James Sr.?" asked Matthew inquisitively.

"Yes, we met him many years later. He came to Bayside, but he never wanted to plant roots with my father. He said he was happy living his carefree life, but he did offer my father some sage words of wisdom. He advised my father to not look elsewhere for happiness but to thank God for what he already has. I guess my father chose not to take his advice and to proceed with his plan of divorce. But more about that later," said Sebastian.

"So how did your parents meet?" asked Matthew.

"Well, my mother and father were seniors at Eastern District high school in Greenpoint, Brooklyn. My mother, Vanessa, was born in Barranquilla, Colombia, and came to New York when she was nine years old. She came with her older sister, Valeria, and younger sister, Maria, but changed her name to Mary and her baby sister, Cynthia, was born in the Bronx. My mother, Vanessa, was a carefree and happy child who had many friends and taught her sisters and friends to bike ride. She would carry a portable radio to school and both she and her sisters would listen to the songs of Diana Ross and the Supremes while walking to and from school. She even dedicated the song *Reflections* to Paul, her boyfriend at the time. She really loved him and thought she probably would have been happier if she had married him. They had a very strict upbringing, and my maternal grandparents believed in what they called it in Spanish *visitas de sofa* which means supervised living room visits or chaperoned dates which usually consisted of taking out my mom with one of her sisters tagging along.

64

"My mother had just broken up with her secret boyfriend Paul who went to the air force because my mother was compelled to turn down his marriage proposal. Paul, one day, went to my mother's apartment to ask my grandparents for permission to marry my mother, but they emphatically refused and even slammed the door in his face! They said he wasn't good enough to marry my mother. He was a smart guy who came from a very religious family that was highly revered in the neighborhood, but I think it was because he was Puerto Rican and my Colombian grandparents felt he was beneath them. Some South Americans look down on Puerto Ricans and it deprived my mother of what could have been her chance at happiness with a man whom she truly loved and vice versa. My mother met my father at the annual feast of the Giglio at Our Lady of Mount Carmel Church in Williamsburg.

"It was July 1970 and the song *What does it take to win your love? By Junior Walker and the All Stars* Was playing on the airwaves, and it came to be my father's song to my mother. They met there on a warm early July evening and talked for over two hours, and my father and mother were quite smitten with each other. My mom had to run home with my aunt Mary so as not to miss curfew as my maternal grandparents were very strict and might have sent out a search party to look for them," said Sebastian.

Matthew wrote intently as Sebastian was describing his father and mother's romance.

"My father finally proposed to my mother in late 1970 as they prepared for a summer 1971 wedding, but they also faced a few obstacles along the way. Grandmama met my mom and originally was unimpressed as she thought my mom was plain, but then she won her over by calling her mom. My father and mother had to go to marital catechism a month before the wedding, but my mom's aunt Hilda decided my mother and father only wanted to fool around with each other instead of taking religious instruction seriously.

"Aunt Hilda was my grandmother's older sister and had great disdain for her family because they were as she referred to them as the 'mechanic's family'. Aunt Hilda was a professional teacher at an exclusive boarding school in Bogotã, Colombia.

"Aunt Hilda looked down on my grandmother, Gabriela, and her family, and tragically, both she and her husband, Andres would be murdered by two thugs who stole their money and bludgeoned them, years later.

"My father was not having any of it and said he threatened to cancel the wedding as he did not need to put up with this childish nonsense. My mother was sick with a very bad cold and told my father her parents would not allow her to go with him to catechism. My father told me she was crying and as he walked down the stairs my grandfather, Anibal, who had slicked black hair like Ricky Ricardo stopped my father from leaving and told him to take my mother to catechism. He scolded Aunt Hilda and told her to mind her own business as my mom was his daughter and he gave her his blessing to go with my father.

"They did go to religious instruction that evening And were married on 5 June 1971. This also cemented a new friendship between my father and grandfather, Anibal," said Sebastian.

"So, your parents actually pulled it off and got married. It was also good that your father had a new ally to help and believe in him," said Matthew.

"Suffice it to say, my grandfather got the son he never had, and my father got another father with whom he could make new father and son memories. And they had been inseparable ever since. Fortunately, my mother did find happiness with my father and loved him very much, but I don't believe she ever truly got over her boyfriend, Paul, but she was aware of the obstacles that would have prevented her from marrying him. Years later, I asked my mother if she had any regrets about not marrying Paul, she said no because if she had married him than she wouldn't have had me for a son. Of course that made me very happy to hear and I was determined to do everything I could to make her happy." said Sebastian.

Chapter 6

Sebastian and Matthew now turned to new topics that pertain to Sebastian's formative years and his memories of his beloved grandparents and parents while living together in Bay Terrace. Sebastian decided to put on a Luciano Pavarotti album to set the mood for this very topic.

"So, Mr. Devereux, why don't we now discuss some of your memories of living in your grandparents' home in Bay Terrace while you were growing up?" asked Matthew politely but resolutely.

"Well, as I explained earlier, my grandparents sold their English Tudor in Hollis Hills which was beautiful but not large enough for all five of us in which to reside. My parents and grandparents spent quite a long-time visiting realtors and looking at beautiful homes, but none of them was quite right. That is until we came upon this majestic Victorian house on the edge of Bay Terrace. It had everything including a guest house, huge yard, finished and furnished basement with a wet bar, and six bedrooms.

"I was ecstatic because I was going to be able to have my own large bedroom! What a joy for a child! My grandparents were pleased because we were all going to be together, my parents were in complete agreement so long as it was in Queens. Everyone came out winning in the end... or so we thought," said Sebastian coyly.

"Would you care to elaborate on that, Mr. Devereux?" asked Matthew.

"Well, for the first three years we really enjoyed living together. Grandmama and Mom got along very well, and she saw my mom as a second daughter. Grandmama had her own ideas on child-rearing as it pertained to me, but she understood and never tried to usurp my parents' will on raising me, but her opinions were mostly welcomed as my mom highly respected Grandmama and Poppy Rocco.

"As a matter of fact, most people in our family respected Grandmama's viewpoints and often asked for her opinions on a wide variety of issues. Some, of course, didn't care for her candor, but others did. I remember seeing people in both our immediate and extended families sitting around Grandmama to ask for her opinions on anything they were dealing with and she'd usually give them advice that worked well for them. I was proud to have a grandmother who had so much wisdom and was highly respected by her family and community," said Sebastian.

"It sounds like your grandmother was a guru of sorts. So how did your grandparents impact you personally?" asked Matthew.

"Well, during the first three years that we lived with them I felt secure because I had wonderful grandparents who were two allies and friends working on my behalf to help me to have a good childhood. They did precisely that in that they made sure I had everything a well-adjusted kid should have such as friends, get-togethers at the house, parties in our basement such as birthdays, first holy communion, and even graduation from grade to grade. Grandmama often told me that both, she and Poppy Rocco were like 'angels' on my shoulders.

"My mother nor I saw anything wrong in that although my father could always be counted on to render an opposing viewpoint. He truly resented that Grandmama and Poppy Rocco doted on me as he said it would ruin me emotionally and psychologically. That may have been a valid viewpoint, but the only problem was that he offered no viable alternative to show me he was proud and loved me. His new law practice kept him busy all the time and whatever free time he had he would usually use for his weekend band rehearsals with his friends to whom he referred as his 'brothers in music'. I often remember feeling sad and a bit resentful of this, but thankfully, I had my mom, grandparents and few friends from school," said Sebastian pensively.

"I remember when I was in the first grade, I wasn't into sports at all as most of the other kids used to play t- ball and basketball, but then I developed a great love for musical theater. I would watch musicals on television on Saturday nights and then asked my mom one day to take to me to see a Broadway show.

"My mom and grandparents discussed it and decided to take me to see *Snow White and the Seven Dwarfs* live at Radio City Music Hall when I was six years old. I had just begun the first grade. The only condition I had to meet was to do well in school and I kept my part of the bargain so off we went to see the show in early January 1980 as I had received tickets to the show from Grandmama and Poppy

Rocco for Christmas. My father was upset about it and refused to be a part of it as he was busy with work anyway. So, my grandparents, my mother, and I went to a Saturday, January matinee show, and it was the best 90 minutes of my life!

"I recall being so frightened at the prospect of the mean wicked witch coming out into the audience in pursuit of Snow White! I remember cowering in fear and hiding my face behind my mom and grandmama. They both lovingly comforted me and to my great relief Snow White lived, married Prince Charming, and lived happily ever after. My grandparents bought me the album of the musical soundtrack along with a few souvenirs from the show," said Sebastian.

"Wow! What did you feel as a music lover being in the audience of that great show?" asked Matthew.

"Matthew, it was like being in the most magical place one could ever visit! From the moment we entered the auditorium, you could smell the magical perfume of the upholstery with the beautiful set designs in the formation of a magical castle carved into the walls on both sides of the theater. It was truly magical... the lights, sets, costumes, and of course the singing helped to make for an afternoon of sheer enchantment for a 6-year-old boy and his family. After it was all over, we went to have an early dinner at Rosie O' Grady's.

"I remember my mom had a delicious rib-eye steak, while my grandparents had fillet mignon steaks and I had a kid steak dinner. The food was wonderful as I recall, but I was dying to get home to play my Snow-White record from the show. We embarked on the express bus on 6th Avenue and arrived home 45 minutes later. Naturally, as soon as we got home, I ran up to my room to play my newly beloved soundtrack record. As I recall, I played it until it was time to shut it off around 10 p.m.," said Sebastian laughingly.

"So, that was your first musical theater experience? Was this what inspired you to want to sing later or were there other shows which inspired you?" asked Matthew.

"Well, it certainly was my first musical show and truly enjoyed it as a child, but later on, I came to discover other shows which truly ignited a flame within me to sing and perform. I recall my mom and grandparents wanted to take to me see another musical. This time we went to see the show *Annie* on Broadway and I really enjoyed that show because I loved the New York ethnicity of the people whether they were as rich as Daddy Warbucks or as poor as the Hooverites who poured out their lament for having made the grave mistake of supporting then-President Herbert Hoover.

"Ironically, when I first started in musical theater years later, I was cast in the role of one of the Hooverites singing in this catchy sarcastic song seemingly praising but ultimately criticizing President Hoover for what he had done to the country from their viewpoint. I remember singing along with Annie played by Andrea McArdle as I was mesmerized by her beautiful and powerful voice. I could also say I admired Dorothy Loudon singing the role of Miss Hannigan especially when she sang *Little Girls* and *Easy Street.*

"I remember we went to see this show on a Friday night when I was in the second grade and again my father was absent. It just seemed we had already gotten used to his absence during such events in my life. But I digress," said Sebastian.

"So now that *Annie* helped to catapult you to a place of pursuing singing in shows as a child, what were some of the shows you participated in while you were in grade school?" asked Matthew.

"Well, I mostly sang in chorus in shows such as *Peter Pan*, *Sound of Music*, *King and I*, and *The Wizard of Oz*. My grandparents and mom were very supportive of me, but a couple of times, I was tapped by directors to sing in a few smaller roles which I thoroughly enjoyed. Grandmama was very supportive of me and insisted my aunt Shirley, cousin Deborah, and other members of my family would come over from Nassau County to see my shows," said Sebastian laughingly.

"I remember Grandmama organizing for all of us to go back to the house after my shows to have dessert and coffee for the adults and milk for me and my younger cousin Nick. My father was noticeably absent as he was not close to my aunt Shirley and was not pleased that I was singing in these performances. He would purposely stay away until at least 11 p.m. so as not to have to run into any awkward situations.

"My grandmother would confront him about it the next day and it would turn into an argument about my grandparents *allegedly* spoiling me and nurturing talent which was not present. You see my father was a very talented and highly gifted musician. He was a highly successful lawyer by profession, but he would play with his band on weekends or whenever he had free time and came to expect thunderous applause after he played the organ, piano, bass guitar, and accordion. He felt I didn't have talent as a child.

"As a matter of fact, he described it as people being kind to me on the surface but laughing at me rather than laughing with me when I would attempt to play the piano or sing. Now, I'm the first to admit I could not play the piano as a young child, but I certainly could sing in chorus and even in smaller parts in plays. My father would politely thank people whenever I was paid a compliment by strangers or family, but he would then reply by taking credit for having passed along a small portion of it down to me but did so grudgingly," said Sebastian.

"Thankfully my mom and grandparents were very supportive of me in all of my artistic pursuits. They didn't necessarily believe I would sing on Broadway or the Opera, but they felt it was good for me to pursue my artistic endeavors in order to help me to be less shy. But even when I wasn't performing in school plays. I spent a lot of time with my grandparents. I remember a time when my grandparents took me to Cunningham Park and I wore a bright-red one-piece denim overall so they could notice me wherever we were in case I got lost as I used to love to run everyplace I went. I was a runner.

"I remember getting separated from my grandparents and feeling panic-stricken as I didn't know how to get home. This was way before cell phones were invented and didn't have quarters to call home. Fortunately, my grandparents found me, and they were relieved and angry with me at the same time.

"I certainly couldn't blame them and I certainly wouldn't blame them now, but I was glad we all found each other that day for fear I would have been left behind just like Grandmama was left in the park by her mother when she was around my age. Grandmama's father, Yener, asked her mother where Rita was, only to be told she was left in the park as she grew tired of trying to find her and would look for her the next day. Great Grandpa was furious and made his wife turn around and go back to the park to find her. As it turned out, Grandmama was at the police station wearing a policeman's hat and eating an ice cream cone," said Sebastian laughingly.

"Wow! I'm glad your great-grandfather made his wife go back and find your grandmother," said Matthew.

"Yes, you and I both. My grandparents were very responsible and caring people. They made sure I was always safe in their care and my mother knew it. She didn't trust me with just anyone. Years later, I used to travel to visit Grandmama Rita and Poppy Rocco when they had condos in Sarasota, Florida. This was after my parents got divorced and went their separate ways.

"We were like the three Musketeers as we got along extremely well, and they truly were second parents to me in every way. I will always love and honor them in every way and want people to know how truly special and remarkable they were. What I'm truly glad about is that my mom got along beautifully with them too and she thought of them as second parents and would often have talks with them about any life-changing decision she and I would have to make... not for their permission but for their guidance, and they were truly honored to be thought of that way," said Sebastian.

"I remember my mom; grandparents and I went to see the movie *E.T.* When it first came out in the summer of 1982, we had such a nice evening together, and it was one of the last carefree days I remember enjoying as a child. I remember that August of the same year I would play with my friends down the block, go to the beach with my mom and cousins, and then enjoy the evening with my mom and grandparents.

"We would often have mini-barbecues on Friday and Saturday nights and my father would sometimes join us when he wasn't so busy with his lawyer duties and musical pursuits. But then I remember one night my father got all dressed up wearing a fancy Versace sport jacket and nice pin-striped red and white shirt and designer jeans. He said he had a business cocktail party and was going alone as he didn't think Mom would enjoy such an environment. He said it was better for my mom to stay home with us rather than to be bored at a boring lawyer cocktail party.

"This was the beginning of the end for my parents' marriage and the beginning of our family woes. As my father grew in popularity at his law firm the less we saw of him and when he wasn't working he was either at his company sports club or practicing with his band," said Sebastian.

"How did your mother deal with your father's prolonged absence from home?" asked Matthew.

"It wasn't easy for her but slowly she came to terms with the fact her marriage was on the rocks but wasn't about to surrender without putting up a fight. My mom felt it would be a good idea to pursue marriage counseling. My mom somehow convinced my father to go to marriage counseling but every time the counselor suggested he make more of an effort in their marriage such as attending more family events or even taking a family vacation with his wife and son which he did when our last couple of family vacations were in Massachusetts and Virginia.

"The first family vacation with his family went well but the last one to Virginia went south when we were in Bush Gardens Old Country. My father walked way ahead of us and he picked arguments with my mother. It got so bad that he even got into an antagonistic row with my grandmama, Rita. As I recall we drove home in almost utter silence except for what was strictly necessary. This was two weeks before I would start my ill-fated third-grade year. More information to come on that!" said Sebastian.

"It sounds to me that your parents were headed toward a separation or divorce at this point," said Matthew.

"It was more like a separation at first but then my mother had a wifely premonition that my father had the wandering eye. As it turns out she followed him one night with Grandmama and they waited for him outside of his law office, and half an hour later, they saw him coming out of his office arm and arm with a red-head lady who looked like the actress Susan Hayward. My mother said he was looking over his shoulder every few seconds for fear he'd be discovered with another woman.

"Grandmama was mortified to think her son would do something so contemptible but she put her hand on my mother's shoulder and offered her condolences and full-fledged support to my mom. Grandmama suggested for my mom not to confront him about it for my sake but Mom said she would have to as she could not share her bed with a man who would cheat on her. It would be like giving her blind consent to what he was doing but she said she would confront him in her own way. My mother at this point was very naïve to marital infidelity as she was raised by parents who believed in marital fidelity and family unity," said Sebastian.

"How did your mother finally deal with it? Did she confront your father?" asked Matthew.

"My mother did confront my father one day when they were alone but kept denying it and when my mom gave specifics of when she saw him with the redheaded woman he became indignant about it and decided he was leaving her. My father stuck around for another few more months before he decided to move out to live with the woman who worked as a secretary to one of the other lawyers. Our problems were just beginning, and for me, it all started in the third grade," said Sebastian.

Chapter 7

"So, by this time your parents were approaching a separation… where did your father move to while they were separated?" asked Matthew.

"Well, after contemplating on the repercussions of moving in with his mistress, he decided to not leave her until he was officially divorced from my mom. He moved into the guest house in the backyard as it was vacant since great grandma passed away in 1981. My parents avoided each other, and I started third grade in early September 1982. This was the year from Hell for me!" declared Sebastian boldly.

"Would you care to further elaborate on that?" asked Matthew.

"Well, I had a teacher named Eleanor Tarantella who by this time was probably in her early 60s although she looked much older to me. She was not a very tall woman, but she held herself in a way that was intimidating as if she were a spider or predatory beast ready to devour her prey in one swift stroke. The kids all nicknamed her 'Mrs. Tarantula' but certainly never to her face.

"At first, she seemed to be no different from any other Catholic school teacher at that time but then eventually she would show me why she earned the nickname 'Mrs. Tarantula'. One day we were going over Math problems and that was always my weakest subject and I guess I had a more difficult time than most in my class. I kept getting it wrong and suddenly Mrs. Tarantella screamed at me like a vicious harpy and would not let up on me. I didn't know how to react to that as I was not used to being yelled at by anyone else. She embarrassed me by telling me I was a slow dim-witted excuse for a pupil.

"At that moment, I was feeling shaky, nauseous, and anxious. I asked Mrs. Tarantella to allow me to use the restroom, but she refused. What's more, she continued to pursue her quest of terror without the slightest intention of letting up on me, and at that precise moment, I threw up all over myself and on my desk. My fellow pupils all broke out in huge laughter and pointed their fingers at me mockingly. Mrs. Tarantella was outraged and began to yell at the top of her lungs. She didn't expect this reaction from me and ordered me to go to the restroom and clean myself. How does an 8-year-old boy clean himself after he vomited all over himself?

"Yet, somehow, I cleaned myself sufficiently enough to be able to go to the nurse's office and ask to be sent home. The nurse called my home and my mother was there and got dressed fast and came to pick me up. When my mother saw what had happened, I insisted I wanted to go home and never return to school again as I was mortified!" said Sebastian.

"So, what did your mother say? Did she make you go back to school that day?" asked Matthew.

"In view of what happened she decided to let me go home but after I took a shower we were going to sit down and have a talk. Fortunately, Grandmama was out with my aunt Shirley in Nassau County as she was helping to take care of my cousin Nick so my aunt could go to her appointments. Since we were all alone, my mom and I talked about what had happened, and for me, it wasn't easy to admit that as a child I was now facing unchartered waters. This should have been a joyous time in my life, but it wasn't.

"I was facing my parents' own separation and inevitable divorce and now I was in the clutches of a sadistic teacher who enjoyed making me suffer. My mother was empathetic but still told me I had to return to the third grade; otherwise, I'd be afraid to face any problem. On the surface this made sense but when a sensitive 8-year-old boy is being told to go to the slaughter like a sacrificial lamb, it is not the easiest cross to carry. My mother and I agreed we would not tell anyone else about this... especially Grandmama lest she march right to the school, confront Mrs. Tarantella and say the same thing her mother told Miss. Coombs when she soiled herself in class as a child. We didn't want any trouble of that nature and it would have attracted even more negative publicity as people talk in school.

"Most assuredly, people did talk especially during the PTA meetings. My mom overheard a group of parents in a huddle talking about me as the 'vomiting boy' who can't deal with the pressures of third grade who should have gone to a special school for kids with psychological problems. My mom went over to them and rebuked them for being gossiping hens who got pleasure at the misfortune of others.

81

She politely but firmly advised them to be more concerned with their own children's affairs in school rather than mock her son for his own temporary challenges," said Sebastian.

"So, after you went back that day, did things improve with Mrs. Tarantella What happened after your mom confronted those parents at the PTA meeting?" asked Matthew.

"Naturally, the parents weakly tried to cover their tracks but to no avail as my mother wasn't having any of it. Another mother whose son was also in my class was timid like me and she shared with my mom her concerns about Mrs. Tarantella. My mom and Mrs. Morelo, whose son was Joey, became good friends after talking about both of us and our struggles in school. Sadly, things did not improve for me... at least not at first. I would vomit in class almost daily it got so bad that Mrs. Tarantella ordered for the custodian to bring a pail and place it next to my desk. I was beside myself and not sure how to maintain my composure considering these new events.

"But then I sort of got revenge on Mrs. Tarnatella. We were discussing more advanced Math problems and I was still having trouble in school and she became so enraged at my 'stupidity' that she came right into my personal space and I vomited all over her! The kids were laughing loudly, and Mrs. Tarantella ran out of the classroom yelling 'I've had it with him!'

"Her other third grade school teacher colleague came over to find out what had happened, but the other kids all yelled that Sebastian threw up all over Mrs. Tarantella. Mrs. Cariello was holding back her laughter but then ordered all the kids to read quietly until Mrs. Tarantella returned. Mrs.

Cariello motioned for me to come to her and when I did, she put her arm around me and advised me to go to the boys' bathroom to clean myself and then go to the nurse's quarters to call home.

"As it turned out, my mother was not home at that moment, but my father was in the main house and when he was told what had happened he said he'd come with a change of uniform for me but was not bringing me home. 25 minutes later my father showed up with a change of uniform for me. He took me to the nurse's bathroom and told me 'to be a man' and stop vomiting. I'm not sure if he even knew what was going on but he made it quite clear he was not Mom and would not be manipulated by my tears and vomit to remove me from the situation. I pleaded with my father, but he turned a deaf ear to my pleas and told me he was going to work now, and he'd see me later to discuss it further.

"My father looked at me with such disgust in a way I was unaccustomed to being looked at by my father. Mrs. Tarantella had to go home after that fiasco as she was covered in vomit from head to toe. I did spend the rest of the day in class and we had a substitute teacher for the rest of the day and even the next day as Mrs. Tarantella decided to call out sick from embarrassment.

"I can truthfully say I enjoyed that day and a half of school. My father never spoke to me that night he only spoke to my mother about my being coddled and that Mom and my grandparents were responsible for my emotional state of being. Furthermore, he said he had washed his hands of me and what I would probably become in the future," said Sebastian.

Did your grandparents ever find out about what was happening to you?" asked Matthew.

"Yes, they did, and they were angry that they had not been told about this before. Grandmama was at the supermarket one day and she was approached by one of the parents of one of my classmates, I think it was Marie Venestro and she saw Grandmama and told her all about what was happening to me but not in an empathetic but tantalizing and condescending way.

"Grandmama was furious and told Mrs. Venestro to mind her own business and further went on to tell her to keep her husband at home as he had the 'wandering eye'. Grandmama confronted my mother and father about what was going on, but it merely turned into an exercise in arguing and blame assigning by my father toward everyone else. My father had heard enough and took his car keys and got into his car and drove off probably to visit his new clandestine girlfriend.

"My mother and grandparents decided they would speak to the principal and Mrs. Tarantella about my problems with her. My mom called my school principal Sister Nora to set up a conference family teacher/principal conference on Monday night, but I was not to be present," said Sebastian.

"So, what happened at the conference? Did your grandparents attend and did they express their grievances and concerns?" asked Matthew.

"They most certainly did, and Mrs. Tarantella curiously was not present. I think Sister Nora felt it was better for her not to be in the same room as Grandmama for fear they would have a 'Holy War' on school grounds! My grandparents were well known throughout the parish and all the officials were familiar with my grandmama's temper when provoked. My mom told me it was a productive meeting and Grandmama and Poppy Rocco also expressed their great disappointment and anger over what was happening with me.

"Sister Nora, true to form, completely empathized with my mom and grandparents and decided to change my classroom and she introduced Mrs. Cariello to them to see if they would agree to allow me to change over to her class for the remainder of the spring semester. Mrs. Cariello couldn't have been nicer, and my mom expressed her concerns and discussed her upcoming divorce from my father. Mrs. Cariello completely understood and assured my family I would be in very good hands with her. Grandmama was skeptical, of course, but she was willing to give her the benefit of the doubt.

"My mother was very candid about her concerns for me and the trauma I endured because of Mrs. Tarantella. She further explained that she had met with her privately before the final vomiting incident one on one to discuss the problem but Mrs. Tarantella was not at all moved by our situation. She simply dismissed my vomiting issues as mere manipulation and that I should learn to grow up and be a man. My mother was completely taken aback by this reaction.

"What made it worse was that my father went AWOL as he had a nightly band rehearsal to attend. Mrs. Tarantella said she also had a musician husband who would often abandon them for his own musical pursuits but even with that admission Mrs. Tarantella was not moved and went

85

further by advising my mother not to change my class as it would only prolong my emotional immaturity, and then she sent my mother away as she had other parents to meet with that evening, but before that she threatened I would probably be left back to have her for another year. My mother knew this was not going to work and given these new developments my mother knew it was time to take action," said Sebastian.

"So how did Miss. Cariello convince your family to allow you to transfer to her class?" asked Matthew.

"Mrs. Cariello and Sister Nora continued to assure my family I would like to be in her class and she would love to have me as one of her students. At this point, there was a lot more smiling and nodding in the room. Sister Nora acknowledged how important the Calabrese and Devereux families were in this parish community as my grandparents donated generous sums of money to the school and church community and Grandmama reminded Sister Nora of this fact.

"My mother concluded the meeting by saying she would discuss it further with me and would let them know by the end of the week. Sister Nora and Mrs. Cariello agreed, and the meeting ended amicably. After mulling it over my mother and grandparents decided that I should be transferred immediately to Mrs. Cariello's class for the remainder of the spring semester which would be from February to June.

"My father, upon learning of this was outraged, but my mother said that he showed no concern at all about me and that I needed a mature parent to make decisions that would benefit me. My father did not want to hear any more criticism of his parenting style and walked away from the argument. To me, it was strange that he walked away from arguments with my family when it pertained to me as he was a shark in court for his clients. He roared like a lion when it came to me but then went out like a lamb, I guess it was because he wasn't interested in winning those arguments," said Sebastian.

"How did Mrs. Tarantella take the news about your transfer to Mrs. Cariello's class?" asked Matthew.

"Let's just say Mrs. Tarantella was called into the office the same day my mother called to let Sister Nora know the family wanted me to be transferred into Mrs. Cariello's class. Mrs. Tarantella was very angry and protested the decision. Sister Nora explained that I came from an important family in the community and that it would be the best thing for all parties concerned. Sister Nora knew that the school did not want to lose me and more importantly my family as generous donors.

"It was settled and that following Monday morning I was to report to class 3-A. I walked into the classroom and nobody knew me there and I even made a couple of nice new friends that same day. Mrs. Cariello introduced me as a new student from another school so as not to give away my identity as the 'vomiting boy' from Class 3-B," said Sebastian.

"So how did everything turn out in Mrs. Cariello's class?" asked Matthew.

"Everything turned out very well, it was like night and day! I still needed help with math, but I was able to get private tutoring at home and my grades improved dramatically. Mrs. Cariello was aware of what was going on in my personal life with my parents and she was very empathetic and helpful when she could be. Make no mistake, I still had to work hard in class but at least I was dealing with a reasonable teacher and not an angry harpy tormenting me all day long," said Sebastian.

"How did you end your year in third grade and how did fourth grade work out for you?" asked Matthew.

"Well, I ended third grade with an A average in Mrs. Cariello's class and was even placed on the principal's list but sadly my yearly average was a B due to my poor grades in Mrs. Tarantella's class.

"The summer was not easy for me because I still had to have tutoring to prepare me for the fourth grade at my mom's insistence. It served me well though because I did extremely well in Mrs. Reilly's class. She was a kind and soft-spoken woman in her early 50s and was firm but fair. I made the principal's list again for both semesters and things could not have gone better for me academically but emotionally things were hard for me that I had to see the school psychologist twice a week just like when I was in third grade. I had to work hard to overcome Mrs. Tarantella's torture. This time we were discussing my parent's upcoming divorce. My mother was also forced to get a job and six months after filing an application, she was finally called by Fordham University to work as a part-time secretary in their Admission office.

"Thankfully, she did well in her job but knew she wanted to be closer to home, so she applied for a CUNY job and was called six months later to work at Queens College. She worked for one of the science offices as a full-time secretary," said Sebastian.

"How was your collaboration with the school psychologist?" asked Matthew.

"It went very well thankfully, but we worked weekly to figure out what was causing me to vomit every day in Mrs. Tarantella's class and we concluded that it was a combination of my parents' marital woes and arguments. I confessed that my father was very angry with the family and even accused me, his son, of causing their marital break-up.

"I recall a time that my grandparents asked me how everything was going in school and I said everything was fine, and at that precise moment, my father walked in on our conversation and I meant to say my father discussed something with my mother, but I mispronounced it and came out as disgusted. My father slapped me so hard across the face that there was a tiny streak of blood on my cheek. I guess he thought I said my father was disgusted with my mother, but I was very young and trying to expand my vocabulary, but it cost me a huge slap.

"Grandmama was angry and yelled at my father. He told her to stay out of it and he sent me to my room while they continued arguing. My father later came to my room to apologize in his own way by saying he was sorry he hit me but that I had caused him to lose his temper needlessly.

"My father learned how to save face by apologizing for his initial reaction but to justify his actions he'd assign blame to the other party for precipitating his negative reaction. Fortunately, he never hit me again, as I recall, but he did wound me emotionally by using manipulation and guilt as his choice weapons in his arsenal. I'll explain this more in detail later," said Sebastian.

"So, tell me more about your parents' divorce. Can you recall when it happened and what it meant for you and your family?" asked Matthew.

"Well my parents, as I was told, had started divorce proceedings in early autumn of my fourth grade which was early October 1983 and my parents appeared in court on 19 June 1984. My mother says my father sneered at her with an evil fiendish look of glee because he thought he had gotten the last laugh, but little did he realize he wasn't just hurting my mom but also me his 10-year-old son.

"What made it even more painful was that my mom had just lost her father my grandfather, Anibal, a week earlier from a heart attack but he had carried a lot of anger in his heart due to my parents' divorce. My grandfather really loved my father and he always looked forward to the times they would share together on weekends during the early years of my parents' marriage. He was so proud of my father for passing the bar and graduating from law school that he would brag about him to all his friends and customers at work. They would talk for hours about anything and everything!

"But as my father succeeded and climbed the ladder of success, he avoided more people and only wanted to be associated with his intellectual peers and band mates. He would refer to them as his 'brothers in the law and band' and I remember overhearing him say that years later when I went to see one of his gigs. I felt so sad that his only interest was in complete strangers and so-called friends who could and did turn their backs on him at a moment's notice.

"Sadly, my father never learned to make the right kind of friends and invest in the right people like his family. Oh, how I envied my cousins Leslie, Eddie, and Nick because they had fathers who invested in them in every way, but I am glad for their sake because now they are doing well in life. Leslie is married, has two beautiful daughters, a fine husband, and a beautiful and happy home in Oyster Bay, Long Island. Eddie became a captain in the police force in Atlanta and Nick my paternal cousin followed in his father's footsteps and became a successful lawyer," said Sebastian.

"I'm sorry to learn about your grandfather, Anibal's death," said Matthew.

"Thank you, Matthew. Well, before he died my grandfather called our home to speak to my father to get his side of the story about why he wanted to divorce my mom, but he would not take his call.

"Shortly afterward, my grandma Gabriela also called to speak to my father but he said to her bluntly he didn't speak Spanish and then hung up the phone. My grandmother was struck dumb by this reaction and told my mom she felt betrayed. Grandmama Rita and Poppy Rocco, of course, felt awful about what was happening and tried desperately to convince my father to not divorce my mother or me, but he said he had already made up his mind and wanted his freedom. My mother at this point had already resigned herself to accept his choice and consented to give him his precious divorce so he could be free and live with his mistress.

"My mother, thankfully, already had a full-time job with Queens College and was getting on her feet financially so we could make the eventual move out of my grandparents' house. My mother had to get a good divorce lawyer to represent her case so a very good friend of hers from Fordham University in Manhattan suggested my mom contact a well-known and highly respected lawyer named John Goldman who was excellent in his field and he gladly took my mother's case.

"My mother was naïve about what she and I were worth so she just told him to get for us what we needed in child support but he liked my mother and fought to get her 300.00 a month which was considerable in 1984 but my father put up so many protests to rectify this 'travesty of justice' as he called it.

"The judge was irritated by my father's 'arrogant and condescending insults' toward my mother that she decided to award her 400.00 a week. From what my mother told me my father was fiercely angry and said he'd appeal it, but it never materialized. What's more, my father had to pay for half my school tuition until I graduated from high school. I can tell you it wasn't an easy time, but the Lord gave us the strength and grace to go through it and come out stronger and wiser for it.

"My mom would read the Psalms every night after we had dinner and I went to bed. She says it gave her comfort and strength and believes we were given a double portion for our troubles. My mother says she had never again doubted the Lord's goodness and faithfulness," said Sebastian.

Chapter 8

It was now 5:30 p.m., and Sebastian and Matthew were well into part two of their interview but Sebastian asked Matthew if he'd like to have Mrs. Alba prepare a snack/dinner while they worked? Matthew agreed and Sebastian called Mrs. Alba to prepare sandwiches and beverages so they could continue working as he knew Mrs. Alba used to leave for the night at 7 p.m.

"Mr. Devereux, how would you feel about working until 10 p.m.? If you like, we can take tomorrow off to rest, and we can then pick up on Thursday where we left off. I have to work in my home office tomorrow but would like to continue on Thursday. I am not sure if we'll be finished by then? I know your mother is coming home on Saturday, and I wouldn't want to infringe on your family time," said Matthew considerately.

"Don't worry, Matthew. My mother has decided to postpone her return until next Thursday. So, we do have some time to work together, and I have another week and a half before I must return to rehearsal for my upcoming concert. I am eager to complete this project with you," said Sebastian.

"We'll continue to work then and stop at 10 p.m. Agreed!" said Matthew enthusiastically.

"Mr. Devereux, you spoke of your parents' divorce and how it personally affected you. How did your grandparents take it?" asked Matthew.

"Well, my maternal grandfather passed away a week before my mother had to go to court to sign the divorce papers. Grandmama and Poppy Rocco were distraught that we were leaving.

"As a matter of fact, they pleaded with my mother for us to stay living with them but my mother knew such an arrangement could not work in the long run as we had to be able to stand on our own four feet. It hurt both of us very deeply to leave them, but my mother assured them we would all still be close and promised them we'd visit them weekly. We would visit them on Friday nights for dinner and tell them everything that was going on in our lives.

"I finished fourth grade at St. Robert's and then transferred to St Nick's where my cousin Leslie attended school. We moved into my aunt Mary's house where we rented her basement apartment. It was such a descent into a new reality that we could no longer enjoy the joy of living with my grandmama and Poppy Rocco. I remember calling them every day for the first month sometimes two or three times a day but slowly I became accustomed to our new lives living as tenants rather than owners.

"My grandparents couldn't take living in their large Victorian house without us, therefore, they decided to sell their house almost two years later. They sold their house and moved into a beautiful huge apartment co-op complex overlooking the Bay Terrace shopping center," said Sebastian.

"How was life living in your aunt Mary and cousin Leslie's house?" asked Matthew.

"Well, we certainly had fun. For me, it was like living with my sister rather than my cousin. I didn't see too much of her during the summer as my mother and I went back with my aunt Cynthia who came back to New York for my grandfather, Anibal's funeral. Her husband, my uncle Alejandro was stationed in Hawaii and was a lieutenant in the U.S. army.

"I remember being so excited to fly on an airplane to Hawaii with my mom, aunt, and two cousins. In those days I wasn't afraid to fly and it was an 11-hour flight which I didn't want to end. We had a nice time going to the beach and visiting sights like Pearl Harbor. We also went to see the Don Ho show and took a day trip to Maui on an old propellered plane! That was a stimulating experience… to say the least!" said Sebastian laughingly.

"So, tell me more about life with your cousin Leslie and family?" asked Matthew.

"Well, we were in fifth grade together but in different homerooms and classes which I think was a good thing so we wouldn't have any conflict of interest being cousins and all. Leslie and I were close in our personal lives but never interacted with each other until school dismissal time at 2:30 p.m. We would sometimes do homework together but once my mom came home from work, we each went our separate ways to spend time with our own families," said Sebastian.

"The following summer we decided to have a Florida vacation for three weeks. My cousin Leslie and her parents drove down to Florida on a Saturday morning and my mom, Grandma Gabriela and I flew down on Eastern Airlines to join them that Monday afternoon. I remember before we left the apartment I was so excited about going on this trip and remember the Mc Gruff the Crime dog commercial coming on the airwaves at 6:30 a.m. it was about a junior high school girl being approached by a stranger in a car. I believe this commercial triggered insecurity in me that caused me to fear being kidnapped or hurt in some way.

"Fortunately, I didn't allow that to deter my good time with my family and as I recall we had a beautiful flight to Jacksonville, Florida and I remember seeing my cousin waiving from the indoor terminal as were parking at the gate," said Sebastian.

"While we were in Florida, we visited my mother's aunt Hilda and her husband, Andres, who lived in Palatka in a mobile home. We didn't stay long there and embarked two days later to Orlando, followed by Tampa and Clearwater. We stayed in an efficiency motel and I became friends with the manager's son, Jason, who was around my age.

"While we were on Clearwater Beach, we saw a fin sailing through the warm waters and my Grandma Gabriela screamed 'Tiburon, el fish! el fish!' and my mom, aunt, grandma, cousin, and I all ran toward the warm sandy beach while my uncle Stachu was frozen with fear as all he could do was look out at us from the Gulf of Mexico. If it weren't serious at the time, you couldn't help but laugh. The natives tried to calm our fears telling us what we actually saw was a dolphin, but my family didn't believe it and made us leave the beach immediately!" said Sebastian laughingly.

"I also recall we traveled later to Ft. Lauderdale and rented two apartments at the Seaview efficiency motel a couple of blocks away from the beach and we had more fun experiences together. I was walking down the street and came under this lush thick green palm tree and found what I thought was a caterpillar, but it really turned out to be a thick green piece of vine that fell off the tree.

"I decided to make a pet of it and wrapped it in a small blanket and fed, changed its diaper, and carried it around with me everywhere I went even in the shower. I insisted Brandy, my caterpillar have its own seat at the table and, of course, I could always count on Leslie for support. She would giggle while Abuela Gabriela would make fun of Brandy and would insist I get rid of him or she'd throw him in the trash!

"I made sure I kept an eye on him everywhere I went, that is until that fateful day when I would discover him 'dead'. Abuela Gabriela took 'Brandy' and crushed him in the luggage and said to me mockingly, 'You see there is your pet!' I discovered 'it' was never real to begin with, and it was nothing but a mere vine that was now cracked in two. That was a very sad moment for me," said Sebastian sadly.

"My abuela, Gabriela, had to leave shortly afterward as she had to take care of her unemployment requests as in those days one had to appear in person to claim his/her own unemployment check. We decided to take a one-day cruise to the Bahamas as a family. For the most part, we had a very nice time and the night entertainment was well worth the trip as a Brazilian girl was singing and I got up on the dance floor to try and dance by myself right near the stage. It was a memorable night. Leslie, my aunt Mary and uncle Stachu all left a day before we had to take our plane home.

"I remember we said our goodbyes the night before as they left for New York at 5 a.m. Mom and I spent our last day in Ft Lauderdale on the beach and I even had a T-shirt with an iron-plastered image that read 'I love My daddy this much' with arms wide open hoping to surprise him when he picked us up at the airport that afternoon. Sadly, It left no impression on him whatsoever but I awkwardly accepted it and did my best not to slip into self-pity," said Sebastian resolutely.

"That sounded like quite a vacation you all took together. Do you recall any other memories with your cousin Leslie?" asked Matthew.

"Yes, I remember Mom and I had moved out of their house and the following year my cousin was placed in an awkward predicament by my aunt Mary and Mauricio Vargas' mother, Gloria. Mauricio was in the seventh grade with Leslie and his mother thought it would be a fine idea for both Leslie and Mauricio to go out on a date together.

"My cousin Leslie emphatically refused and protested to the highest extent, but my aunt Mary managed to convince her that it would be for the good of harmony in the PTA as Mauricio's mom was vice president of the PTA and my aunt wanted to fit in well with her. I was already living in my abuela, Gabriela's house at this point and Leslie called me one night and begged me to be a chaperone on her date. I almost peed in my pants from laughter. I couldn't believe what I was hearing and asked her why she wanted me to go along on her date. She said she did not want to date this guy; therefore, I would be the perfect 'third wheel' to serve as a spoiler.

"At that moment, I didn't know if to be flattered or insulted but, I decided to help Leslie in her quest to keep young Mauricio at bay. The catch was that Mauricio was not to know I was accompanying Leslie right until we met at the movie theater in Forest Hills. I remember He wore a greyish denim jacket and Leslie also wore a light blue denim jacket and sported a very high 80s hairstyle and I wore a green denim jacket. When we arrived at the theater, Mauricio's reaction was priceless, he was struck dumb when he saw me accompanying Leslie.

"Clearly, Mauricio was upset but he tried to maintain his composure, but he really was smarting from the blow to his pride. I remember we saw the movie *Hello Again* starring Shelly Long who comes back to life from the dead. If you were to photograph this visual, the camera would start with a shot of Mauricio's outraged reaction slowly panning to my confused and embarrassed facial expression slowly panning to Leslie sitting mortified and fearfully way to the right of her seat ready to depart the theater at a moment's notice.

"Honestly, I felt bad for Mauricio because he was looking forward to having a hot date with Leslie only to have his wings clipped by Leslie's geeky cousin... yours truly. As soon as the movie ended, Leslie was pulling on my arm motioning for us to leave and Mauricio was also in a hurry to get away from this fiasco of a date. My aunt treated me to pizza for services rendered over and beyond the call of duty. I asked them to drop me home afterward because I had to prepare for a Social Studies exam the next day which, fortunately, I aced in spades.

"Leslie and I did not hang out as much shortly afterward but she did return the favor when I needed a date for my eighth grade dance and accompanied me and my classmates couldn't believe I could get a pretty girl like Leslie to accompany me to the dance but after we got there she danced with another guy who liked her named Edgar but it was fine because I explained to him that Leslie was my cousin and wanted to accompany me as a cousin and not a date. They exchanged phone numbers but didn't date for very long. It was probably better that way for both in the long run. Once we got to high school Leslie and I saw even less of each other, but I understood as we were very different personalities who evolved in different social circles.

"I will always treasure my early childhood memories with Leslie and Eddie, and we both wanted to marry her, and he would taunt me that Leslie preferred him over me. I tried to be happy for him but deep down inside it bothered me. Putting that aside, I love Leslie and Eddie and wish them both the best in their lives," said Sebastian reminiscently.

"So, tell me about your life while living with your Grandma Gabriela?" asked Matthew.

"Well, at first I had a difficult time understanding Abuela Gabriela partly because I didn't speak much Spanish as my father forbade me to learn Spanish as he wanted me to speak perfect English. But once my mother and I had moved into my abuela's house I had to be able to communicate with her properly, therefore, she taught me painstakingly slowly, but I eventually started learning and she quizzed me on my multiplication tables in Spanish. I can recall her saying '*seis por ocho... ocho por seis... doce por trece y trece por doce*' to confuse me but then I caught on to her tricks and finally was able to keep up with her.

"At first, I thought Abuela was prudish, bossy, and narrow-minded, but then I came to understand and love her for her traditional ways and began to incorporate those traits into my life. Abuela told me about her childhood in Colombia and she explained to me that she was a tomboy and loved to play sports as well as study. Abuela even went so far as to confide in me about how she met Abuelo Anibal and how she played hard to get before she allowed him to date her. She told me he used to visit her father's bodega where he would sit down and have a beer with his friends.

"Abuela worked in her father's bodega and made it abundantly clear that she liked sober and decent men. He assured my abuela that he had good intentions and would never behave ungentlemanly with her. It took quite a while to convince her but slowly but surely, he did. She told me he eventually courted her for a couple of years, and they got married and moved to Barranquilla where my mom and my aunts; Valeria and Mary were born but Abuela always aspired to come to the United States to start a new life of opportunity.

"My abuela worked hard for several months going to the Colombian and U.S. consulates to legally immigrate with her family to the United States while my Abuelo Anibal worked hard in New York to prepare for the arrival of my abuela, mother and two aunts. She single-handedly brought forth her family from a comfortable unexciting life to a working but exciting life raising their daughters with good hard-working work ethics and patriotic values. My Abuelo always loved his country, Colombia, until the day he died, but I was told he always respected this country and all she stood for. They were good hard-working people, but I had a different relationship with my abuela than with Grandmama and Poppy Rocco, but I learned to respect and admire her.

"At this point, I stopped playing tricks on her and dragging my poor younger cousin Eddie into my schemes and truly learned to have a relationship with her as a young adult. I now thank Abuela rather than mock her," said Sebastian repentantly.

"So, what was happening in your mother's and your life at this point?" asked Matthew.

"Well, I was in eighth grade and had a strict teacher named Mr. Manggiacavalo who was a portly and intimidating man who had a great deal of influence and ran the eighth grade like a tight ship, but he did good for the school and meant well. He liked me as I recall and always made the honor roll while I was in his class. He even paid for my school trip to Florida as he insisted, I needed to be a part of it so I went on the class trip to Orlando on a bus with 40 other brash kids but I enjoyed the trip and it gave me an opportunity to get away from home as my mom was dating a very persistent guy named Javier Mauricio who was also Colombian.

"My mom told me she met him at Queens College who called her on the phone for help with his financial scholarship. She moved heaven and earth to make sure his scholarship paid for his studies in full and then we paid...

royally. He persistently pursued her at work, and she says she tried to discourage him, but it made him even more persistent which we have paid forever since," said Sebastian fearfully.

"So did your mother agree to date this man?" asked Matthew.

"More than that, she actually allowed him to meet me at my abuela's house to take me out for a snack and I felt very uncomfortable accepting his invitation as I did not know this man but after I called my mom about it, she told me to accompany him as she sent him to meet me. I was really unnerved by this and had a foreboding feeling that this man was going to do us a lot of harm and sadly I was right. But more about that later.

"I graduated from eighth grade and got accepted to Holy Cross high due to my father's influence. He taught a Business law class for them one semester several years ago as a guest lawyer and they were appreciative of his services, therefore, they allowed me to attend on a partial scholarship as an act of Catholic charity, but I will always be grateful to him for taking command of this situation," said Sebastian.

"This is when our lives were about to change forever as my mother decided that she and I would move in with Javier Mauricio into a rental apartment complex in Fresh Meadows, Queens. I had just turned 14 years old and we were now living together all three of us. It was the beginning of one of the most difficult chapters in our lives as everything comfortable we knew before my parents' divorce was now finished and we would struggle as we had never struggled before.

"Thankfully, the neighborhood was very nice, it had a beautiful Bloomingdales on the main avenue and the grounds of our community were well-manicured and adorned with small and fancy boutiques. I thought we had moved to an upper-class Westchester rural community but in Northeastern Queens. The drawback was that I had to sleep in the living room while my mom shared her bedroom with this most undesirable predator who had more on his mind than wanting to be a part of our family... much much more," said Sebastian solemnly.

At this point, Mrs. Alba brought sandwiches and beverages to both Sebastian and Matthew so they could eat and continue to work hard on this biographical project. Sebastian put on Martha Argerich's Rachmaninoff piano concerto three followed by Tchaikovsky's piano concerto CD concert from Berlin. Matthew seemed to be impressed with this CD selection. Both ate their food while they enjoyed listening to this wonderful artist at play while contemplating everything they have discussed until now.

Chapter 9

"So, when did you move to your new apartment? And what happened during your eighth-grade graduation ceremony and party... I believe you mentioned something briefly about it during our short dinner break?" asked Matthew.

"Well, we moved to Fresh Meadows, Queens on 18 June 1988, literally a day after my graduation ceremony but I couldn't help my mom move that day because Grandmama Rita and Poppy Rocco had catered a party for me in their apartment. My aunt Shirley, cousin Nick, Poppy Rocco's sister, brother-in-law, and my father who made a brief but unforgettable cameo appearance were all there.

"Leading up to that, my father was in a very bad and sour mood the night before at my graduation ceremony. My aunt Shirley took a picture of the two of us and you could tell he wanted to be on Mars instead of at this event. After the ceremony was over, I saw Grandmama Rita and my father having an argument across the street from the church. I said goodbye to my mom and her family as I had to join my grandparents to spend the night at their apartment over the weekend for my party," said Sebastian.

"So, did your father show up at your grandparents' apartment the next day?" asked Matthew.

"Initially, he wasn't going to attend as he felt his pride had been hurt by grandmother inviting my mother to the party. He was of the mindset that once he divorced my mother, all contact should have come to an end between my mother and his family but what he failed to realize was that when children are involved, that complicates things. He wanted his new girlfriend to become the new darling of the family, but my grandparents simply could not warm up to her as she was an eccentric woman who had a lot of hang-ups, she was a germaphobe, who could not tolerate germs or children for fear they were carriers of germs. But I digress, he was angry he felt he was Grandmama's second choice for the parent to be at my party but Grandmama invited both my parents to be present.

"Grandmama loved my mom and wanted both to be present but he couldn't handle it and considered it a slight to be asked to be in the same room as my mother. Sadly, my mother couldn't be there that day as she had to move our belongings to the new apartment but considering everything that was going on, she was glad she wasn't there. Personally, I wish she had been there instead as my father after being 'begged' as he described it came with such a terrible attitude that he started an argument with my aunt," said Sebastian.

"My aunt Shirley, cousin Nick and the rest of the guests arrived that afternoon and within five minutes my father greeted my aunt by saying 'hello pest', and at that moment, she ran out of the apartment into the hallway while being pursued by my father like a bat chasing its prey. Grandmama Rita and my aunt's mother-in-law, Lois, ran to see what was going on only to stumble upon a huge shouting match mostly by my father.

"It then turned into my father yelling at Grandmama for favoring my aunt and never taking his side on issues. My aunt Shirley was crying as she was confused as to what had brought on this cavalry charge of hate toward her. He went back and forth with Grandmama only to have Poppy Rocco boisterously yell at them from the front door to grow up and stop acting like childish babies.

"Grandmama, true to form, yelled back at Poppy Rocco to get back in the apartment and keep things calm until she returned with everyone. The arguing continued for another 15 minutes and after it was all over my father returned to get his spring jacket and say goodbye to all of us as he was not going to be a party to this 'climate of hatred and hypocrisy'. He told me he'd call me later, took off, and walked down the stairs on eight flights as he didn't want to wait for the elevator for fear the family would try to talk him out of leaving but no one did.

"We made the best of the situation, but not before Poppy Rocco scolded Grandmama for allowing such a spectacle to take place in the hallway for fear of the neighbors' reaction.

"Grandmama could care less what the neighbors said and yelled it out to an eruption of laughter in the room. The caterers finally arrived that afternoon, but they were 45 minutes late, and Grandmama was not happy about tardiness. That was a pet peeve of hers but thankfully the food was delicious we were served baked ziti, meatballs, sausage, pot roast veggies, and a huge salad. They set it up buffet style, so everyone got up to serve themselves. Dessert was brought by my aunt Shirley as she had a wonderful bakery not far from where she lived in Nassau County.

"My cousin Deborah came a little later but still got to enjoy some of the food and more importantly the great conversation with Grandmama and Aunt Shirley including the huge argument between my father and aunt. We celebrated until around 8 p.m. as Poppy Rocco had to drive his sister, Marie and brother-in-law Joe home to Brooklyn and my aunt Shirley had to drive home with her family home to Nassau county, but my cousin Deborah decided to spend the night with us, and we continued great conversations into the late night," said Sebastian.

"So, did your father ever call you that night?" asked Matthew.

"Yes, he did but we only speak briefly as neither one of us was up to a long conversation with each other. I felt ashamed of my father for starting an argument with my aunt. I felt as if though he used his childhood issues with my aunt as an excuse to cover up bigger issues; some of which he had with me.

"To this day, I strongly believe he was jealous of me, and for the light of me, I cannot understand why. He is a great musician and lawyer, he has a gift with words, and he helps people who need an advocate to defend them, but instead, he chooses to use his gifts negatively and destructively toward his family.

"I remember one day, we were sitting in his car one afternoon when we were alone together, and he was quiet and in a solemn mood when out of nowhere he looked at me and told me something I would never have expected to hear from my own father. He just looked at me probingly as if he were looking into my own soul and said, 'you could never really love anyone, could you son?' At that moment, I was speechless and struck dumb as if I had been silently and surprisingly punched really hard in the stomach.

"I stumbled and asked him why he would ask me such a question, but he merely looked at me with his lawyerly icy penetrating eyes that he often used while interrogating witnesses and merely responded that it wasn't an opinion but a fact. I wanted to cry and go home that day but not wanting to sound like a crybaby I just told him that he was wrong and didn't appreciate his question as politely as I could. He further elaborated that I merely used people and went where the action was. From that statement, I deduced he was venting because he resented Grandmama and Poppy Rocco for doting on me as they had while I was growing up.

"To this day, I felt he was jealous and in competition with me because he felt he didn't get the beautiful royal treatment from my grandparents that I received. You see, I never nagged or even asked my grandparents for anything, but they wanted to be good to me. What kid wouldn't love that, but I genuinely loved and cherished my grandparents because I could be myself around them and not feel I was being judged or scorned by the cynicism of others," said Sebastian.

"How old were you when your father told you those things in the car that day?" asked Matthew, greatly surprised.

"I would say I was about 15 years old just before he stopped speaking to me for the first time but more on that later," said Sebastian.

"So, what was happening with you in your new living arrangement with your mother and Javier Mauricio?" asked Matthew.

"Well, let's just say it was a very difficult transition for me as I had to sleep in the living room as my mom could only afford a 1-bedroom apartment at the time. As it was, they didn't, initially, want to rent my mom the apartment but my mom convinced them we were not a charity case as she worked full time for CUNY and could afford to pay them the rent on time and in full.

"But living with Javier Mauricio was difficult from day one as he was ordering both of us around telling us how he wanted things done and it would be done his way only and there was no option for any other way. I remember I had not yet started high school and had to kill my summer by going outside and walking around on hot summer days. I remember I would eat breakfast and then leave by just saying I was leaving to Javier Mauricio as he was not working at the time.

"I only relied on an allowance my mom gave me as I was too young to get a part-time job yet and I'd go to the local movie theater to see matinee films and then go to Carvel and buy myself a shake as I was very skinny in those days and could afford an occasional shake. I would wait to come home after 5 p.m. once I knew my mom was home and when I didn't go out, I'd visit my grandparents when they weren't in Florida or stay at home watching television all afternoon," said Sebastian.

"What did your father think of this new living arrangement of yours?" asked Matthew.

"He wasn't happy about it, to say the least, and called my mom at work to vent his frustration but there was nothing he could do about it as he himself had a new wife who was no better than Javier Mauricio. My mother would ask me to try and get along with him, but I said I couldn't because he was too bossy, and I didn't like his nomadic ways. He was what I would call in Spanish a 'picaflor' who pollinated many flowers with his flattering and flirtatious words with many women while he was in a relationship with my mother," said Sebastian.

"I remember we went to Amish Country in Lancaster, Pennsylvania one weekend in August and I was trying to guide him so we could get there faster but he stubbornly chose to go his own way and, in the process, got us lost. It was too late to continue traveling that we had to sleep in the car instead of already being in Lancaster so we could enjoy our time there.

"I remember we got into arguments and it got so that my mom yelled at both of us to stop fighting that I completely ignored both of them until we arrived there the next evening and by the time, we could eat in one of the family-style restaurants we could only get left-overs. It was one of the worst weekend trips I ever had in Amish Country.

"I remember we were driving home from Amish Country and my mom and Javier Mauricio got into a big argument that he actually jumped out of the car in protest. My mom pleaded with him to get in the car but yelled that he wouldn't under protest. I felt bad leaving him stranded that I suspended my distaste for Javier Mauricio and asked him nicely to get back into the car. He surprisingly accepted and we drove home in silence. I chose to not be a part of any other trips that involved Javier Mauricio as I was older at this stage of my life," said Sebastian.

"So, what particularly repulsed you about Javier Mauricio?" asked Matthew.

"Well, he was very revolutionary and anarchistic and challenged the United States on all of her virtues. He was a self-proclaimed socialist and said he had no use for this country except for what he could get from it. He was a sociology major in college from what my mother told me and he wanted to help this country embrace a socialistic economic policy and wanted to constantly challenge us because we didn't espouse that globalist viewpoint.

"I was happy to agree to disagree, but he wasn't going to let me get away with that form of 'pacifist surrender' as he called it. I remember he tried to bait me by bringing up incidents that involved the United States 'stealing' Panama away from Colombia and other accusations that I lost my composure at that moment and told him to get lost.

"Javier Mauricio was very insecure when it came to my father that he forbade me from calling my father from the apartment. He told me I would have to go downstairs to a public phone, as cell phones did not exist back then, to call him. My mother sadly, went along with this and to this day I could never understand why," said Sebastian.

"What else about Javier Mauricio turned you off about him?" asked Matthew.

"I didn't like the way both he and his family used my mother to do favors for them without even saying please or thank you. They were like gypsies who thought they were the finest of Colombian society and his mother and relatives looked down on my mother by making innuendos about her appearance meanwhile my mom looked great and was working out at the gym on the elliptical machine and bike but they considered her to be beneath them and always referred to Javier Mauricio's ex-wife, Rosario, as being a beautiful beauty queen back in Colombia 'something other women weren't' referring to my mother and how Rosario had missed Javier Mauricio.

"To me that was low. It's one thing to have a relationship with your ex-in-law but to brag about her to put down your current daughter-in-law goes beyond the pale, given all that Mom had done to help his mother Eduvina. I remember the first time we met her she wore a Joan Crawford 1940s hat the Hollywood stars would wear with very high stilettos that a woman in her 60s had no business wearing at that age.

"I remember Javier insisted my mom refer to her as Mrs. Eduvina and eventually wanted her to be called mom, but my mom drew the line right there and said she'd call her Mrs. Eduvina but not mom as she only had one mother and only would call Grandmama mom when they were alone together but quickly had to change that once she was involved with Javier," said Sebastian.

"Did your grandparents ever meet him?" asked Matthew.

"Yes, they did a few times and Grandmama's impression of him was that he was 'flighty' and looked like an opportunist and she was right because as soon as he got his U.S. citizenship then it was 'Adios Javier' and that suited me just fine. I did, however, feel bad for my mom because she really tried hard to make her marriage work with him, but he didn't know how to appreciate her, and what's more, he didn't understand he was not my father and didn't understand the dynamics involved with being a stepfather.

"He wanted to, as he saw it, 'make a man out of me' and take over where my father failed to mold me but when you are a stepparent you can't just take over and try to undo the child's upbringing and personality. He had a very machismo third-world mentality when it came to rearing boys; I remember he even forced me to get under a car one day to do an oil change which I had no desire to learn but he was bold and pushy about it causing me to cry in front of my mother's family. He did not understand or care that I was not the type to be manhandled in that fashion. I was a very sensitive and artistic child even then before my budding talent with singing and music.

"Was your father supportive of you during your difficult time living with your mother and Javier Mauricio?" asked Matthew.

"Sadly, he was not very supportive at all. On the contrary, he used me to deliver direct messages to my mother back and forth. Specifically, he wanted to sell his half of the land he had purchased with my mother during the early years of their marriage. He told me to tell my mother he demanded she send him a bank-certified check for 5,000.00 within 30 days or he'd take my mother to court and sue her for it.

"My mother said this was brought on by her asking him to help pay for half of my braces for my teeth. When asked if he had harbored any ounce of guilt because he would be hurting his ex-wife and son in the process, he merely said we could afford those miscellaneous expenses without any help from him and it was good for our own self-sufficiency.

"Miraculously, my mother came up with the money to pay him off and bought us some much-needed peace though at a high cost at the time," said Sebastian.

"How was your time in high school when all of this was going on?" asked Matthew.

"My time in high school was a mixed bag of academic success and stressful bullying by certain classmates who hated me for being sensitive and artistic. I recall a time when two guys named Patrick and John followed me one day as I was walking to catch my bus. They caught up with me and started punching me, and after they got their jollies, they walked away laughing at me. I managed to regain my composure and walk to catch my bus and went home and ran into my bathroom to clean myself and remained quiet about it until now.

"I guess the only consolation was that there were no witnesses to add to my humiliation. Then there was another instance when I was being bullied by a bigger kid named Ralph. He would torment me in class in front of others and it was impacting my studies and well-being.

"I remember Grandmama and I visited her sister my great aunt Millie in Massapequa Park, Nassau County We took the railroad out there and Great Aunt Millie noticed I was painfully quiet and could tell something was bothering me and when I opened up about my situation with Ralph, she was very compassionate and understanding. Grandmama wanted to visit my school to confront him but Aunt Millie interjected and told Grandmama that would be harmful and counterproductive.

"She wisely suggested to befriend this bully, and he would more than likely lay off and become my friend in the process. Do you know, it actually worked and we became pretty good friends for the remainder of our time in high school? And when I sang in high school plays, I became pretty popular with my classmates. I even tutored Ralph in Spanish to help him do pretty well so that he could successfully complete three years of high school Spanish.

"We both mutually benefitted because Ralph passed high school Spanish and I was left alone by him and all other bullies because he gave them strict orders to leave me alone.

I will never forget Aunt Millie's great advice and happily reported to her the great news shortly afterward," said Sebastian triumphantly.

"Were you bullied by many kids in high school and what did you do to cope?" asked Matthew.

"Fortunately, I was not bullied by many kids in high school... thank God, but the few bullies who did make life difficult did leave an emotional scar causing me to have trust issues with my peers. I do remember being laughed at in the gym locker room in high school because I wasn't well built like my peers.

"It became so hard for me that I even ditched gym class a few times and when I was in gym class, I would try to hide by the cardio machine section to make it look like I was being active. I hated to be called upon in class because the other kids would make fun of my high speaking voice which made me sound like a girl but thankfully it served me well in music. This all made me become very self-conscious about my masculinity or lack thereof as well as my poor hygiene as a teenager and it didn't help when my father would make derogatory insinuations that I wasn't well-groomed. In retrospect, I believe he was right but he could have been more kind in his remarks.

"I remember one time we were watching a classic movie called The Big Country and there was a scene when Burl Ives tells his son played by Chuck Connors to 'take a bath sometime' and my father took that movie line and directed it toward me. I honestly didn't know how to respond to that so I just remained silent which is a coping mechanism I had learned to master quite well as a teenager. So, to answer your original question, I was pretty much alone in dealing with my private tormentors both in school and in life but I overcame by the grace of God.

"As it turned out after my father quoted that movie line to me, it forced me to take stock of myself and make necessary changes to improve my image, therefore, I thank my father today even though at the time it was difficult to hear," said Sebastian solemnly.

"Was college a major improvement in that part of your life?" asked Matthew.

"Thankfully, my college years were a dramatic improvement in my social relationships! I was well-liked by my peers and had more friendships, particularly in the college chorus. You might say I was given a second chance at life which I like to think has led to my success in opera today," said Sebastian happily.

"In the final analysis of Javier Mauricio, I wouldn't say he was a bad man but very foolish and misguided in his approach to dealing with a family that was not originally his

117

own. I remember even trying to tell him this one day but he merely brushed it off in his clownish way and just said I was too sensitive and serious or maybe he wasn't serious or mature enough to comprehend this concept? Food for thought," said Sebastian.

"You mentioned during our dinner break that you also have a sister… tell me more about her," said Matthew.

"I have a sister named Rachel and she is many years younger than me. She was born a couple of years before her father, Javier Mauricio, left my mom. My mom told me Rachel used to cry a lot after he left and would cry out for him in the middle of the night but Mom would do her best to console and share all the love her father couldn't give her but she still needed a good father image in her life just like I did.

"My mom would apologize to both of us because our fathers were emotionally and physically absent in our lives, but I certainly understood and am glad I never went away to college because my mom would have been left all alone with Rachel and I could not live with myself knowing that," said Sebastian.

"What was life like for all of you during those years after Javier Mauricio divorced your mom?" asked Matthew.

"It wasn't easy but somehow we made it work. My mom and I worked very cooperatively with each other as I went to college but also worked part-time in clothing and record stores which ignited in me my great love for singing and music. But returning to my sister Rachel, she was a temperamental child and made life difficult for us. The terrible 'twos' extended into her teens which became known as the 'turbulent teens'.

"I remember my mom had to do laundry downstairs one night while I babysat for Rachel and she hated being in her crib and did everything she could to escape it like an 'unwanted prison'. She was very pretty and would say to me 'up... up' and I would reply 'down... down' which only infuriated her more. I did everything I could to entertain her, but she insisted to get out of her crib all the more and when I firmly told her No! She jumped up and screamed in my face a blood-curdling scream to end all screams!

"As she grew older, she and I had less and less to do with each other as we were different personalities that agreed on very little which is to say nothing. Please understand I would always care and love her as my sister, but I really don't like her as a person, and I know the feeling is mutual. When I would ask my mom about this, she said in a diplomatic way that Rachel was insecure and resented our close relationship," said Sebastian.

"What are some of the traits you like and admire about your sister?" asked Matthew.

"Well, Rachel has always been a smart girl and I have always admired her scholastic aptitude and high IQ which was very similar to my father's. As a matter of fact, I have often wondered if my father would have made a better father to Rachel than her own father as they were similar in so many ways. The few times they saw each other before my estrangement from him they used to get along well together and one night before he left our apartment, she stood on top of a footstool and put on his cap, and smiled at him.

"He was enchanted with Rachel and said aloud 'she should have been my daughter' which gave me a feeling of

joy at the time but little did I know how true that statement was as they both had similar ways of dealing with people of whom they disapproved by separating themselves permanently from people they could not tolerate as Rachel and my father would later do to us. I also admire her determination to go after what she set her mind to achieve. I guess I learned I had some of that in me which had to be developed," said Sebastian.

"In the final analysis, Rachel was not in sync with my mother or me. She had no use for Christian traditional peace-loving people such as the two of us who just wanted to get along with everyone and live our lives the best we knew how. It was not beneath Rachel to throw a stone rock in a pool of serenity in order to make her point.

"As she hit her 20s she started going out and not returning home until either very late at night or sometimes two days later. This used to drive my mother crazy with concern for my sister's safety and Rachel knew this but still did it anyway. She felt she had rebelled against ostracizing authority and would never again return to its clutches, but she always got away with things most children never got away with, I guess it is her father's traits that manifested themselves in her life and caused my mother and me to pay for his departure. He often told my mom 'Rachel, my baby will be a lot like me, so you'll never be rid of me completely'.

"At the time, we brushed off those empty threats, but it seems there is a great deal of merit to those stinging words now," said Sebastian.

"So, whatever became of Rachel? Does she still live in New York?" asked Matthew.

"She moved away after graduate school to Philadelphia but then moved to San Francisco to live with friends and possibly a boyfriend. We know very little about her life and I think she wants it that way. I just feel bad for my mom which is why I was more determined than ever to shower her with a lot of love, understanding, and things we could not have in earlier years thanks in large part to the opera chorus," said Sebastian.

"Well, why don't we stop here today and let's meet on Saturday to continue the saga. How would 10 a.m. work for you so we can work the whole day with a few breaks in between and see if we can bring this baby in for a landing?" asked Matthew jokingly.

"I think that could be a fine idea Matthew. As you know my mother has postponed her return to New York as she wants to spend a few more days in the warm and sunny weather of Sarasota," said Sebastian.

"I'd like to cover some more about your estrangement from your father and then would love to discuss your artistic journey with pursuing singing and how it has impacted your life. We will play it by ear and see if we can conclude this biographical interview series on Saturday or next week," said Matthew.

"That would be fine Matthew so long as we have finished by next week as I have to resume rehearsals for my upcoming concert at the end of the month. I'm afraid my artistic hiatus is soon coming to an end," said Sebastian.

"I am confident we will be finished by Saturday if we work the whole day collaboratively," said Matthew confidently.

Matthew put his notebook in his tote bag and smilingly said good night as Sebastian walked him to the door and closed the door behind him. Sebastian sported a look of relief as he had shared a lot of sensitive material to someone, he barely knew, hoping he hadn't made a mistake.

Chapter 10

Matthew arrived at Sebastian's apartment at 9:45 a.m. and apologizes for being a trifle early but was most eager to get started on what he hopes will be the final chapters of Sebastian's life and artistic journey. Sebastian was pleasantly surprised to greet Matthew and escorted him personally to the den which both men have come to know well. It was Mrs. Alba's Day off so both men decided to have food delivered and Matthew insisted on treating Sebastian as his way of thanking him for his generosity and cooperation.

"Well, here we are again, Mr. Devereux. So, picking up where we left off on Thursday, why don't we begin with what led to your estrangement from your father?" asked Matthew cautiously.

"Well, I don't believe it was just one isolated incident but a series of events which multiplied in intensity and caused a volcanic eruption in both of us. The first time I had just barely turned 16 and Grandmama and Poppy Rocco invited me to spend a few weeks at their condo in Sarasota. They wanted me to stay the whole month with them and my aunt Shirley and cousin Nick but I knew my father was

going to take a couple of weeks off in July and asked me to join him and, of course, I agreed. He was unhappy that I was going to spend even a couple of weeks with them but reluctantly tolerated it with the condition I'd spend a couple of weeks with him at his home in the country.

"I remember feeling sad and anxious about leaving the comfort of Grandmama and Poppy Rocco's home, but they assured me all would be fine. As it turns out I got home very late from my flight back from Sarasota and my mom and Javier Mauricio went to the airport to pick me up as I was forced to take the Raleigh flight to Kennedy instead of La Guardia airport… but the drama didn't end there," said Sebastian.

"Please continue, Mr. Devereux," said Matthew curiously.

"I woke up the next morning and packed my small Snoopy Met Life orange and blue duffle bag determined to get the motor coach to the Poconos but thankfully, my mother insisted that I call my father before going up to the county. He answered the phone and I told him I was already back in New York and was going to take the bus to meet him. His reaction was his 'vintage' James Devereux interrogatory style as he had often used in court while cross-examining someone he wanted to trap. He was silent for 30 seconds and then asked me what day I got home, what time, and why I hadn't I called him as soon as I landed.

"I think he was looking for an excuse for me not to come up to the country as he told me to go back to Florida. I remember feeling a huge hot flush of tension and anxiety flowing from my chest up to my head reminiscent of all the times I had called him in the past from that public phone I

had come to know well, thanks to Javier Mauricio. I was mortified and felt so terribly guilty and he ended the call. His excuse was that he had a strong premonition that I really didn't want to be with him but with Grandmama and Poppy Rocco.

"Sadly, he was right but not for the reasons he put forth but because of his hypersensitivity and I felt like I was always walking on eggshells when I was around him. He said to me to have a nice summer and abruptly hung up on me. I was deeply embarrassed and sad but at the time relieved that I had listened to my mother's advice and called before going up there. My mother said to me that I should return to Florida as my mom was working all day and she knew I didn't want to be at home with Javier Mauricio and they got me a standby buddy pass and I took the afternoon flight to Sarasota. I called Grandmama about it and she was sad about what had happened with my father but delighted I would be returning to Florida to spend the last couple of weeks with them. We made the best of the situation and drove back with them after our vacation was over," said Sebastian.

"Did you both make peace after that incident on the phone that day?" asked Matthew.

"On the contrary, things only grew worse after that as my father called my grandmother once we had returned from Sarasota and he asked her if I was there, and she said yes as we had just come home the night before. She was about to call me to speak to my father, but he told her not to put me on the phone as he was only calling to confirm his suspicions and told her he didn't want to have anything more to do with me. What's more, he told Grandmama he

had washed his hands of me and no longer had a son. This was the day James Devereux verbally disowned me as his son," said Sebastian vulnerably.

Matthew looked stunned as he was hearing those words it was something surreal out of a 1980s melodrama like Mommie Dearest starring Faye Dunaway as she disinherited her children in her will.

Grandmama was left with the painful task of relaying the news to me. Poppy Rocco merely laughed it off and couldn't believe a father would just disown his own son merely because he didn't do something, he wanted him to do? He dismissed it as childish indignation and he was probably right, but we all came to learn that Hell hath no fury like a wounded and vengeful lawyer named James Devereux.

"Would you care to elaborate on how your father expressed his vengeful anger?" asked Matthew.

"Well, he never retaliated with physical violence or anything of that nature, but he did use a more potent weapon that of the poisonous pen. I came home one day from school and came upon an envelope addressed to me with no return address on it. I knew it was from him as I was well-acquainted with his cool and purposeful penmanship and as I opened the envelope, I could feel the anxiety intensify in me like a gnawing pressure in my gut and chest and there it was, he called me all kinds of names and basically told me I was an ungrateful spoiled brat who didn't deserve a grand and wonderful father like him. He said I was easily manipulated by everyone else but him and that I should grow up and become a man before it was too late. He

concluded by calling my mother filthy names and referred to Javier Mauricio as an illegal cockroach who could never come up to his ankles in value.

"As much as I was not a fan of Javier Mauricio and severely disagreed with the way he treated my mom, Rachel and me, I was so embarrassed that such a talented and gifted lawyer and musician like my father could use words of hate and rage in such a contemptible and disreputable way. I felt he had butchered and massacred the beauty of our English language in a way to hurt and destroy people.

"As a child, I remember he helped me with a couple of book reports when I was in fourth grade and he was wonderfully poetic and as a result of his help in writing my assignments I came out with the highest grades in History and English. I remember being so grateful to him for his help that I bought him one of his favorite movies on VHS, East of Eden I think it was and he was very happy about it. I guess it was one of the very few times I pleased him in my life only to be later greeted by an avalanche of subsequently nasty and candid letters," said Sebastian sadly.

"So, did you both ever make up?" asked Matthew.

"We did a few years later as my father had suffered from a bout of pneumonia and Grandmama asked me to talk to him on the phone. At first, I was greatly reluctant to do so, but I did call him, and he reluctantly accepted my call. We did see each other a month later as I didn't want to rush things between us as the trust value had deteriorated between us. We saw each other occasionally, but things were never the same between us ever again. He retired from his law practice after 27 years as he was tired of practicing law and wanted to pursue his musical endeavors

professionally as he had made a very nice nest egg for himself. He moved with his wife Consuelo to somewhere on the east coast of Florida, I think it was near Boca Raton as he didn't care for the west coast of Florida.

"He came back to visit New York to tie up some loose ends before moving permanently to Florida and I recall we went to a pizzeria in my neighborhood. I met him by the express bus stop right in front of my apartment building and he only had a couple of hours to spare so we agreed to eat in that pizzeria restaurant nearby.

"We went into the pizzeria and ordered our food and were talking when suddenly, out of the corner of his eye he spots a young dirty blonde-haired girl allegedly staring at him, and her boyfriend was seated opposite her. My father yelled at her to stop staring at him and would get up and make her stop if he had to. He then became like Robert DeNiro in an Italian mafia movie such as *Goodfellas* and threatened the boyfriend to not look back or get up or he'd 'finish him'.

"Fortunately, they didn't want any trouble and looked away from him and paid their bill, and left the restaurant. I was as red as the tomato sauce on my plate and asked my father to please stop causing a scene while this altercation was going on, but he refused to listen. I was about ready to run out of the pizzeria when finally, cooler heads prevailed.

"We left the restaurant and my father decided to board the express bus to go back to Manhattan as he had to meet his wife to go out with friends. He reluctantly hugged me and told me to take care of myself and not be a stranger. I knew this was code language for something but didn't know

he was going to disown me again, but only this time, it was permanent," said Sebastian.

"I remember sending my father a beautiful Easter card and called him a few times to see how things were and the last time I spoke to him he sounded like he didn't want to talk to me and merely said he was tired and would call me later, but later never came and then Grandmama told me one day he washed his hands of me again and never wanted to speak to me no matter what happened.

"Oh, how I had come to know those words so well I remember telling Grandmama I was fine with that but to leave well enough alone regardless of her best intentions. She understood, but it saddened her to see her family was coming apart at the seams. Grandmama was a wonderful mother and grandmother and could not help but feel betrayed that her best intentions had failed, but I assured her they hadn't," said Sebastian.

"So, since that happened you never saw him again for any reason?" asked Matthew.

"I did see him two more times but not directly. What I mean by that is we were both present at both Poppy Rocco and Grandmama's funerals years later, but we did not interact with each other at all, therefore, I don't count those events. He completely ignored me and I dutifully reciprocated," said Sebastian.

"So, what else was going on in your life at this time after your estrangement from your father?" asked Matthew.

"I remember feeling very solemn one day at home when I called Grandmama and asked if we could meet to go to the movies as I wanted to see the movie *Used People* starring

129

Shirley MacLaine, about a highly dysfunctional widow and her equally dysfunctional family.

"We met on a Saturday afternoon in January for an early matinee at the Forest Hills Midway. As the movie was playing a very young Frank Sinatra sang a lovely song called *The Sky Fell Down* and it really resonated with Grandmama as she was 14 years old and she told me she went to a dance and this song was playing when a young man asked her to dance. She wasn't in love with him, but she loved the song just the same. The whole Rachel Portman soundtrack really resonated with me at a time when I was feeling vulnerable and downtrodden as I had not only been rejected by my father but also uncertain about my future. I hadn't yet graduated from high school and felt very lonely and uncertain about what I should be doing with my life.

"After the movie was over, Grandmama and I grabbed a light snack at a nearby restaurant and we spent the next couple of hours talking about my fears. Grandmama was a great listener and she was well attuned to people's feelings and motives. Personally, I think she would have made a great therapist or anything she set her mind to accomplish. I told Grandmama I loved music and wanted to sing professionally. Her response really shocked me as I thought she would try and discourage me, but she didn't. She advised me to take voice lessons and try to get into the opera or Broadway chorus, but my real love was opera.

"I remember purchasing a vintage early José Carreras recording and I used to sing along with his arias and songs and felt I was training with him even back then," said Sebastian.

"So did your grandmother serve as a catalyst in encouraging you to study voice formally and one day perform?" asked Matthew.

"I like to think so, as Grandmama was a wonderfully inspirational life coach when she believed in the cause you were pursuing, but she was also a realist and she encouraged me to also study and get a proper university degree as she believed like Mom and Poppy Rocco that one has to have a reliable alternative just in case singing didn't work out. I certainly agreed with that notion and pursued English and Creative Writing as my major at Hunter College.

"Fortunately, I did very well and received my bachelor's degree four and a half years later, but the music never left my heart, therefore, I decided to study voice with a teacher at Hunter College's music department. I sang Tamino's aria from *The* Magic *Flute* a German aria by Mozart. She accepted me as a student and at the time charged me 25.00 a week for a lesson. I also studied sight-reading and piano so I could become a more proficient musician. I had already studied six months with Mrs. Mueller before she asked me if I wanted to start participating in voice competitions and I nervously but eagerly accepted and my very first voice competition was at the Steinway piano store on 57th Street across from Carnegie Hall.

"I remember it was a beautiful and sunny spring day and I was called into a special large recital room and had to sing with an accompanist playing at a gorgeous black grand piano. I introduced myself and sang Schubert's *Ave Maria.* I remember feeling so empowered and full of adrenaline as I sang. One of the judges closed her eyes as if she had been

dreaming as I sang. I then sang *It Must Be Me* from Leonard Bernstein's *Candide*.

"After the judges tallied up their votes, I was told I had come in 3rd place out of 50 contestants. Mrs. Muller was well pleased with that classification and frankly so was I," said Sebastian.

"So how did you perform in other voice competitions under her tutelage?" asked Matthew.

"Yes, I participated in a couple of other competitions, one came six months later when I sang at Weill Hall, which is a smaller hall affiliated with Carnegie Hall, and selected to sing Donizetti's *Una Furtiva Lagrima* from L'Elisir d' Amore which is a light comical opera also known as opera buffa.

"I received very nice applause and even a partial standing ovation which is not easy to receive from an audience. I then followed up with It *Must Be Me* from Candide. I received very nice reviews in the arts section of The *Village Voice* which my teacher showed me at my next lesson," said Sebastian.

Mathew was just writing intensely as Sebastian was sharing this information with him not yet looking up to ask him another question.

"I remember Mrs. Mueller asking me if I wanted to now try participating in an all tri-state voice competition, but it would involve traveling to Penn State University at State College. I told my mother about it, and at first, we weren't sure if this was the right thing to do as it was a long-distance trip and would involve driving through mountains and hills,

but Mrs. Mueller was most persuasive in convincing us by telephone and she even arranged for us to travel with another Spanish-speaking mother and her 'snobby' soprano daughter.

"We did travel together and all we heard on the entire trip was how brilliant her daughter was as a singer and that she had her pick of any conservatory in the United States she wanted. My mother and I were seated up front and politely smiled but rolled our eyes when we looked away. They were Argentinian and only had use for other fellow Argentinians and only believed that the best singers and musicians in Latin America came only from there.

"Finally, we arrived after four grueling hours of traveling together and listening to these women brag and we went our separate ways as we looked for our rooms and prepared for Round one of the competition," said Sebastian.

"So, tell me more about the competition, when were you called to sing?" asked Matthew.

"I was contestant # 11 to sing. I was nervous and felt a compelling desire to fight or flee from this experience, but my mother calmed me down and said everything would be fine no matter what and I should just do my best and sing for the Lord. My turn finally came, and I sang *Una Furtiva Lagrima,* I chose this aria because I figured it might bring me a good fortune as it did at Weill Hall six months earlier. I was nervous and regretfully not in the best voice that day. I was eliminated in Round 1, but my mother and I decided we would still take part in the dinner that was offered to honor all of the contestants that day.

"As one could expect, the Argentinian soprano sailed to the next round easily, and her mother was on Cloud 9! Mrs.

Mueller came over to Mom and me and assured us that I sang well and should be very proud of myself. We graciously thanked her for her warm compliments and she then walked away to meet with other students and their families. Shortly afterward, a judge came over to me and he took me aside and assured me he wanted me to advance and felt very sad that I hadn't. He went on further to compliment me on my voice as being a very lovely tenor voice and that I should not give up as he said I had the makings of a very fine tenor in the opera world as either a comprimario or principal tenor.

"I thanked him for his kind words, and he shook my hand heartily and walked away as Mom and I were about to eat our dinner consisting of pot roast with whipped mashed potatoes and string beans for me and rib-eye steak with sides for my mother," said Sebastian smilingly.

"As we were eating my teacher came back and asked if there were two more seats next to us available as this young man and his father were looking for a place to sit and have dinner. I looked up and there was a slightly tall strapping blonde-haired young man with greenish-blue eyes smiling politely. We motioned for them to sit and the next I knew we were conversing, and our parents were also conversing about the competition.

"The young man's name was *Jonathan Di Lorenzo* who is not only a wonderful lyric baritone, but one of my now dearest friends in Opera. We were both very complimentary of one another and agreed to exchange phone numbers at the end of the evening and from that moment on we had cemented a very important and I like to think a beautiful

friendship. I had such a warm feeling of comradery and anticipation of better things to come for me.

"Perhaps, this is what I needed to experience so I wouldn't give up prematurely. We approached the Argentinian mother and daughter and congratulated them on her success in advancing to the next round and wished her well. We explained we could not stay for the remainder of the competition as we had to return home to my then-baby sister Rachel to pick her up from my grandmother Gabriela.

"At first, they sounded annoyed as they were worried about how they were going to get home but then another Argentinian parent whom she met would be happy to wait and drive them home. They superficially said goodbye and walked away within seconds. We had breakfast the next morning and left right after we said goodbye to Mrs. Mueller who had to stay for the remainder of the competition," said Sebastian.

"We left Penn State and decided to visit the nearest super Walmart ten minutes away and we had a ball shopping as it had everything one could imagine! Grandmama would have had a ball shopping here and I even purchased a men's devotional calendar with biblical scriptures and we came to discover that after 9/11 happened we read the devotional for that day and it came from the book of Zephaniah 1:15–16 which speaks of the dark clouds, gloominess, desolation trumpet and alarm against the fortified cities and high towers! It really affected us as that devotional had been written three years before 9/11 actually happened!" exclaimed Sebastian.

"Wow! I'd love to read that devotional calendar entry sometime! So, a great deal of good came out of this voice competition notwithstanding The Argentinian mother and daughter's input. Did she win the competition?" asked Matthew curiously.

"Yes, Lorena DiMartino did win first place as one could expect, but I was happy for her," said Sebastian humbly.

Chapter 11

"So, did you do any more voice competitions after that tristate competition?" asked Matthew.

"Yes, I did but not associated with Mrs. Mueller as I had realized that she had taken me as far as she could, therefore, wanted a change in vocal technique and needed a hiatus from singing. I spoke to Mrs. Mueller a month later and explained that I was pursuing a master's degree and needed ample time to devote to my studies in Spanish. I wanted to perfect my understanding and command of the other language and would return to my voice studies later.

"Naturally, she was unhappy about my decision and even tried to get me to change my mind, but eventually, she conceded my point and never called me back. I did express to her how grateful I was for her tutelage and faith in me, but my decision was based on academic pursuits," said Sebastian peacefully.

"So, tell me more about academic pursuits. Where did you pursue your master's degree in Spanish and what came of it for you?" asked Matthew.

"Well, it took me three years to get my degree as I had to start slowly due to time constraints and mastery of the language in a literary way, but I held my own quite nicely

for someone who was only a semi-native instead of a native speaker. I made very nice friendships with three people who were very complimentary and encouraging of my abilities. When they found out I was a voice student, they insisted I sing for them and once the director heard of this, she insisted I be a part of the Spanish department holiday parties. The professors were very impressed that I could sing and asked me to sing a Spanish song and Zarzuela (Spanish opera) aria. I chose to sing *Granada* by *Agustin Lara* and *No Puede Ser from the Zarzuela La Tabernera del Puerto.* It was a challenging piece, but I put all of my heart and soul into singing it and was received with warm and friendly applause.

"I remember the director Doctora Fuentes and three other Spanish professors came over to huddle around me to tell me how much they loved my voice and would like me to sing during some very important upcoming events including the romance languages and drama departments annual joint concert of literary recitations and music selections. They asked me to sing a Zarzuela aria which I chose *Bella Enamorada from El Ultimo Romantico.* I was on Cloud nine as I could see how the audience connected with me and seemed to truly love the way I was performing as I believe in singing from the soul," said Sebastian.

"What became of these singing opportunities… did it lead to other singing events?" asked Matthew.

"Well, I was focused on finishing up my master's degree and I had another two years until I completed all of my prerequisites, so I took a job working for the college fitness center. You may think that was a strange job for me to take, but I needed the job and still had to pay rent as my

mom and I were the only ones working and contributing to rent at the time. I went to the job interview one Saturday afternoon and I was met by a very tall and stern-faced man named Brendan.

"He never smiled during the interview but saw my limited work resume and my eagerness to work and decided to be 'generous' and give me a chance. I guess his gamble paid off as I learned the ropes and although I didn't look the part, I turned out to be a good pick and he offered me more hours as a result," said Sebastian.

"That sounds fascinating. Tell me more about your time with the fitness center," said Matthew.

"I made friends pretty fast and then I met him one day, his name was Warren Duong, he was only 5'5" tall, Asian, athletic lanky built and loved to strut around the gym like he was an important celebrity. He would enter the gym wearing dark sunglasses, black sleeveless muscle shirts and acted like he was better than everyone in the room, but as soon as Brendan or more lovingly known as *Biff* entered the room, he would stand at attention and insist everyone else do the same... what a brown-noser Warren was!" said Sebastian laughingly.

Matthew laughed heartily at that last statement as he was taking notes. Matthew offered to have lunch delivered so they could eat while they worked, and Sebastian gladly accepted as he was getting hungry. They both agreed to order Italian food from the nearby Italian restaurant, and they delivered the food at 3 p.m., and true to his word, Matthew gladly paid for lunch.

"I worked at the college fitness center four days during the week and one day at HMV music store which now no longer exists in the United States, but it was an oasis for music lovers no matter what genre of music you preferred. While I was there working one Saturday, I waited on a nice dark-haired and olive-skinned gentleman who was inquiring about Jonas Kauffman's latest opera CD.

"We started talking about opera and music and he then shared with me that he was a voice teacher and if I ever wanted to take a voice lesson with him, he'd be honored to take me as a student. I asked him why he would want to accept a new student whom he never heard sing before. He then confessed that he was in the audience of one of the Hunter College cultural events I had participated in and he said he was very impressed with my lyric tenor voice but offered where he could help to find a different way to sing more diaphragmatically to produce a less throaty sound when I sang.

"I was intrigued and took one of his cards to set up an appointment with him. I looked at his business card after I rang him up at the cash register and read his name aloud *Marco Hernandez*? I asked. He then said yes, smiled, and said he hoped to see me soon," said Sebastian.

"So, at that moment, you were on the precipice of entering a new artistic collaboration?" asked Matthew.

"You have no idea Matthew! I set up a voice lesson with him a week later and he had me sing scales up and down for about 20 minutes and I sang a song called *Del Cabello Mas Sutil*, and he accompanied me on his piano while I sang. I felt a rush of euphoria as I sang. He then asked me if I knew the lyrics to *Sole e Amore* by Puccini as I told him I wanted

to sing Puccini operas one day if given the chance. He smiled devilishly while he handed me the piano-vocal score of Sole e Amore which I sight-read as I was singing it. It is based on Act three of *La Bohème*, and it embodies all the raw emotion a tenor could hope to sing and interpret with all of Puccini's raw emotion and lyric beauty.

"For the first three months, all we did was practice scales and sing songs of that bel-canto style. I remember asking Marco if I could sing songs and arias in French and German, but he strongly advised against it as he wanted me to have a more open bel canto sound instead of the closed French sound I had been taught, but he did it in a non-accusatory way as he understood different teachers have different styles and operate from their field of study and training. This made me appreciate him even more and indulged his request for repertoire selection," said Sebastian.

"So, while you were completing your master's degree and working at the college fitness center and HMV, how did you have time to balance everything?" asked Matthew amazedly.

"I did at first, but it had come at a price as I started to experience anxiety attacks and was, therefore, forced to give up my HMV job which I loved, but my doctor said I was burning the candle at both ends. I, instead, focused on my master's degree and working at the fitness center. I, fortunately, received a pay raise and was able to focus on completing my master's degree and still work at the fitness center at Hunter College. Warren started to notice me more than before. He saw me one night waiting for my express bus to Queens and offered me a ride.

"At first, I was reluctant to accept his offer, but he was most persuasive, therefore, I got into his car. As we got closer to home, he asked me if I was interested in having dinner with him at a neighborhood diner near both our houses, I accepted, we went Dutch treat of course, but it was nice talking to him and then he asked me if I had a girlfriend which I thought was an odd question but, wasn't particularly offended by it as it never occurred to me he was trying to find out if I was gay or straight. I said I was single which was and is still true today and he then dropped the subject. He then drove me home and said good night and drove off," said Sebastian.

"Warren and I were never chummy chummy at work, as a matter of fact, he took great pains to show me and everyone else he was not going to show me any special treatment of any kind. He would shake hands and embrace his other friends in the fitness center but would only greet me with grunts of hi and bye or his choice phrase 'later'. I didn't really care as I had so many other artistic and scholastic endeavors ahead of me that I only wanted to focus on those.

"But as time passed, Warren started asking me to hang out with him with nobody else around and he would do strange things like one day sitting on my lap in front of the other guys and they would wolf whistle and jeer and he would play it up flamboyantly, but I would walk away as I did not wish to become the poster boy for Warren's towel-snapping antics.

"I remember another time he stood on top of my lap and because he was slim, I could withstand the pressure, but then I asked him to get off and he did so but looked at me

intensely as I turned around and walked away," said Sebastian.

Matthew kept taking notes as Sebastian further explained how things evolved between them.

"I remember one 4th of July Warren asked me what I was doing that day; I told him I was spending it with my mom at home enjoying the festivities from a safe place. Right then and there, Warren invited himself over to my apartment as he was eager to meet my mother and was expecting a barbecue to celebrate the special occasion. I told him we had planned on keeping it simple and he agreed it could be done including him in our plans.

"I spoke to my mother about it and at first, she was bewildered about it, but she agreed because she wanted to meet a friend who so eagerly wanted to meet her. We told Warren to come after 3 p.m. , but he decided to show up at 1 p.m. I told him it was too early to come up to my apartment, therefore, we could hang out outside until then. He agreed for us to wait for 45 minutes but then wanted to go upstairs. I told him we couldn't because it was too early, but he kept asking 'why?' ... 'why can't I go up there?'. He was so stubborn that finally I just couldn't take it anymore and invited him upstairs.

"My mother, thankfully, was fully dressed but couldn't get over Warren's insistence on coming upstairs. Fortunately, they got along well, and he even brought a beautiful cake with him for dessert. Rachel later that evening insinuated that Warren liked me romantically. I

merely laughed at her, but then I started to put two and two together and it was completely logical.

"Another time he wanted to celebrate my mother's birthday the following year, and we did again, but we surprised her this time. My mother liked Warren, but she never imagined that he liked me romantically," said Sebastian.

"So, it sounds to me like the plot thickens," said Matthew wittily.

"Well, once Warren was promoted as a full manager of the fitness center, he hardly gave me the time of day and just treated me, thereafter, like I was an ordinary employee. That suited me just fine as I had other plans and ambitions to fulfill and did not want any distractions to deter me from my present course. I graduated that June with my master's degree in Spanish and things were going well with my voice lessons with Marco Hernandez. He encouraged me to pursue community theater and opera performance auditions which I did for about a year when suddenly, Marco urged me to audition for the Met opera chorus.

"Naturally, I experienced trepidation at the thought, but he assured me I was ready and needed to earn a good living singing in the chorus. Marco helped me to prepare two Italian arias one of which was *Federico's Lament* from *L'Arlesiana* and one of Alfredo's arias from *La Traviata*," said Sebastian.

"So, what happened set up the setting for me when, and where did it happen?" asked Matthew enthusiastically.

"It was in late July on a Friday afternoon and I was so nervous, but I initially auditioned for the auxiliary chorus as I was told I would have to start there and work my way

upward. I remember getting a message from the Met choral master's office offering me the opportunity to audition as I had already submitted my audition CD recordings of four arias two Italian, one French, and one German.

"I remember assembling with hundreds of other contestants and when it was finally my turn I exuberated warm and positive energy as I sang my first aria *E La Solita Storia from Cilea's opera L'Arlesiana* and I managed to maintain that same level of confidence and open flowing and ringing sound throughout the audition as they only asked me to sing two arias. Of course, the judges were poker-faced as they were expected to be but then they wanted to confirm my contact information for accuracy twice as to make sure they could reach me if called back to audition again. I left that afternoon with great peace in my heart as I knew I had truly done my level best to give my best performance.

"I remember calling Marco later that evening and he assured me that if I had done my best then I had already won. Two weeks later the choral master's assistant called me and told me that I had made it to the main opera chorus! I was ecstatic, she briefly explained all my duties and job benefits that came along with the position.

"Needless to say, I formally resigned from the Fitness Center the following Monday giving them two weeks' notice as the choral master wanted me to get started in late August to be ready for performances in early October," said Sebastian gleefully.

"Wow! How did your family and employers take the news about your departure?" asked Matthew jubilantly.

"Mom was so happy you would think we had won the lottery and in a sense that was true because two years later we were able to purchase this apartment where I now live with my mother. Grandmama and Poppy Rocco were ecstatic as they always wanted me to sing in the opera chorus.

"I remember they invited my aunt Shirley, cousin Nick, uncle Jeff, mom, and Rachel to a big round table dinner at a beautiful Italian restaurant in Brooklyn called Gargiulo. It was such a long drive to have Italian food, but I must admit the food was outstanding and we all had a wonderful time filled with laughter and fine dining. Biff was stoic about my departure, but he wished me well and accepted my resignation.

"Warren behaved strangely and just shrugged off my news as if it were a footnote on the last page of a newspaper in 8-inch font, but I didn't let it bother me. However, later I found out from a friend that Warren took my departure pretty hard and took out his aggression on the fitness center employees. I was told things had gotten so bad that a couple of them snuck up behind Warren as he was asked by Biff to test the plastic tunnel-like obstacle course for the upcoming athletic Olympics because he was the only one slim enough to fit inside of it.

"Suddenly someone snuck up behind Warren and smacked his rear end and shoved him inside while struggling to get out. What made it worse was that someone was filming this for the college athletic video and then they broadcast it for the entire gym to view. Biff was outraged upon discovering the video and immediately confiscated it, but it was too late as it had already gone viral which led to

146

the termination of the guilty individuals, and Warren was mortified which caused him to resign in disgrace. The video had even been uploaded to social media and other people's iPhones, therefore, it was virtually impossible to remove it completely," said Sebastian.

"Wow, that must have been painful and embarrassing for Warren. Did you ever see him again?" asked Matthew.

"Well, I was not happy to hear about what had happened to him as he was after all my former boss and friend for a short time, but I have always wished him well and will always care about him. We did meet one more time after that whole incident, he shared with me that he went into the corporate banking industry and was becoming quite a success in the process.

"I remember we ate at a Paris Baguette cafe one night while we were sharing our success stories, he in the banking industry and I in the opera chorus. As we were approaching his car, I was about to say good night but, Warren then asked to drive me to my car.

"I thanked him but explained that I was only parked on the next corner, but he insisted on giving me a lift and while we were parked, he told me that he was sorry for acting indifferently with me after he was promoted to fitness center manager and hoped we could pick up where we left off. I paused for ten seconds and then turned to him and explained that we had both moved on in our lives; I assured him that I wished him well in his future endeavors but felt it would be wrong to ignore the fact that we had gone down different paths and things could no longer be the same between us. I said, directly, that I did care for him while we worked

together and always would, but it was time for both of us to move on.

"At that moment, Warren looked stoic and sad for the first time since I knew him, and I could see it in his eyes, but I think he knew I was right. As I was about to leave his car, he put his hand on my shoulder and hugged me which really freaked me out, but I reciprocated and the embrace felt like it lasted for several minutes, and just before he stopped hugging me he kissed me tenderly on my lips and then put his hand on my leg and I, in turn, said goodbye. I exited the car feeling lonelier than ever as I knew I was saying goodbye to someone I had really cared for, but I was confident that I made the right decision.

"At that moment, when I entered my car, I played my CD by Andrea Bocelli singing *It's Time to Say Goodbye.* Nevertheless, I could still feel the kiss on my lips and didn't want the feeling to disappear."

"Wow, that must have been a liberating feeling for you when you reached that moment of self-discovery!" asked Matthew.

"Oh, you are right indeed! It wasn't easy, but I knew it was right. After that spectacular scene, I prepared myself full time to sing in my opera chorus roles starting with *La Traviata* then followed by *Rigoletto, Tosca, La Bohème* and *Madame Butterfly.* I tell you, Matthew, a whole new and exciting world had opened for me and it gave me the golden opportunity to watch individual artists at work crafting their art and it served as encouragement for me to perform my very best where God had me at that time.

"As a matter of fact, I believed that the chorus was probably going to be the apex of my career as it had been

almost five years before I was offered a comprimario role which was *Basilio* from *The Marriage of Figaro.* I remember being called by the legendary Maestro Fulgencio Riccardi, himself when he asked me if I would be interested in understudying for the role of Don Basilio.

"I gladly accepted the challenge and one night I was asked to go on for an indisposed comprimario tenor and I sang the role with the loving care with which I had always sung my choral roles and it paid off dividends beyond measure! I still sang as part of the chorus but then was asked to sing *Arturo* from *Donizetti's Lucia di Lammermoor.* It was another small but valuable triumph for me, and I continued to rack up other comprimario roles with great success and was asked by Maestro Ricciardi to be taken out of the chorus and contracted as a regular comprimario tenor!

"This was unbelievable as I had not at all expected this success this late in life, but then again, I was just over 30 years old, principal tenors often make their debuts while in their early 30s," said Sebastian with great relief.

"Did your grandparents watch you perform in the chorus and comprimario roles?" asked Matthew intently.

"Poppy Rocco did get to watch me perform in the chorus and as Don Basilio in Marriage of Figaro and Arturo in Lucia di Lammermoor. Sadly, he lost the use of his legs a year after those two comprimario role performances at the Met and he passed away peacefully in the summer of 2007, I had just turned 33 years old and he was cremated and his urn of ashes was taken to Long Island National U.S. veterans' cemetery where they played *TAPS* because he was a U.S. soldier who served in the Korean War. Oh, how I missed Poppy Rocco after he died, but I was gratified to

know he got to watch me perform and live my dream," said Sebastian solemnly.

"Did Poppy Rocco offer you a musical review of your voice?" asked Matthew.

"Poppy Rocco was a jovial, kind, and generous man in every sense of the word. He was just happy to watch me perform and do something I truly loved doing as his belief was that life was short and one should do what makes one happy. He wasn't a huge opera fan like Grandmama, but he certainly respected and admired the opera arena although he was partial to musical theater shows like *My Fair lady* and *King and I* as he greatly admired Yul Brynner's masterful performance in that role!

"He also liked the way I performed in community musical theater when I sang the role of Max Detweiler from *The Sound of Music* Poppy Rocco once told me that after he watched me perform in that role, he knew right then and there. I'd be a success either in the opera chorus or as a soloist. I only hope he is proud of me from Heaven," said Sebastian tearfully.

Chapter 12

"So, Mr. Devereux, at this point in your career you have sung in a few comprimario roles at the Met and Civic Center, where did your career turn next?" asked Matthew curiously.

"Well, I continued to perform in more comprimario roles such as Beppe in *Pagliacci*, Goro in *Madame Butterfly*, Monostatos in *Die Magic Flute*, and several other roles but then slowly, but surely, I was asked by conductors to essay certain primary tenor roles such as *Don Ottavio*, *Tamino*, and *Nemorino,* and then it finally happened," said Sebastian menacingly as if he were about to withhold very important information from Matthew.

"What do you mean? Oh, come on now you can't leave my readers hanging!" said Matthew playfully.

"Well, I received a call from Maestro Ricciardi's assistant, and she asked me to hold for him as he wanted to talk to me on the phone. I thought I was in trouble as one never received a personal call from the Maestro unless it was something supremely important. The Maestro came to the phone and he told me he wanted to offer me the lead tenor role of Genaro from Donizetti's Lucrezia Borgia which he wanted to stage at the Met. I was very excited as I

have always admired that lyric tenor role and would love to perform under the baton of Maestro Ricciardi. He asked me how fast I could learn it and I gratefully and joyfully assured him I would learn it at lightning speed," joked Sebastian.

"It was the start of the 2010–2011 season, and I opened the season singing Genaro and I was ecstatic as I was about to sing a role many great lyric tenors like Alfredo Kraus and José Carreras among others have sung. I remember the lighting on stage feeling like 1,000 embers burning at the same time, but some of that was due to my own nerves. I really vocalized well that whole morning and lightly sang throughout the afternoon. I was so restless that I got to the opera house three hours before time, but I then relaxed as I saw my colleagues and finally Maestro Ricciardi appear assuring me I'd be fine.

"And so, it went and played even better than the maestro had predicted. All my high notes were there, and my soprano Mirella Giacomo was at her supple success and we all sang our very best that evening," said Sebastian triumphantly.

"Was Genaro the role that launched your primary tenor career?" asked Matthew.

"Well, it certainly placed me on the map and it caught the attention of other conductors who wanted to cast me in lead roles not just at the Met but also throughout opera theaters in cities like Cincinnati, Dallas, Atlanta, Boston, San Francisco, and Miami.

"Shortly afterward, Maestro Ricciardi decided to mount a series of La Bohème performances in November and December at the Met and wanted me to play the role of

Rodolfo! I was completely beside myself as I had been offered the role of all roles!

"When I was 13 years old my grandparents, mom, and I went to the movies one night to see the movie *Moonstruck* starring Cher and Nicholas Cage and I was mesmerized with the gorgeous La Bohème recording with the legendary Renata Tebaldi and Carlo Bergonzi singing Rodolfo! The hairs were standing on my arms and could feel the electricity traveling throughout my body as I absorbed the energy. It was right then and there that I decided that I would one day sing opera and I have never looked back since.

"For the great José Carreras, it was seeing *The Great Caruso* on-screen which helped plant the seed of desiring to sing, and for me, it was seeing Moonstruck while listening to that magnificent recording of *La Bohème.* I remember I was to make my debut and called Grandmama and told her. She was in shock and insisted that a whole row be set aside so that she could invite my aunt Shirley, uncle Jeff, cousin Nick, his date, cousin Debra, and of course, my grandmama and mom were also going to be there. We set aside a whole grand tier box seating them center stage so they wouldn't miss anything," said Sebastian joyfully.

"Tell me about the evening set up the scene for us," said Matthew.

"It was a Saturday evening in December about one week before Christmas and the weather was particularly cold at that time of year, but people still managed to attend performances. My mom was wearing a beautiful royal blue blazer with a black pantsuit and all the emerald diamond rings I bought her way back when I was a struggling

employee working in the Fitness Center and a couple of office jobs I held at that time. Grandmama wore a beautiful black and gold embroidered pantsuit and she had a perm done just to look great for the occasion.

"My aunt Shirley came with Uncle Jeff and cousin Nick who also brought a date. I guess he felt it would kill two birds with one stone because he'd attend his cousin's performance and show his girlfriend a romantically good time at the opera. What better opera than La Bohème?" said Sebastian rhetorically.

Matthew wrote intensely and smilingly as Sebastian described the evening.

"As a matter of fact, my good friend Charuka also came to the Met with her mother, and Marco my voice teacher was there with his beloved wife.

"I remember standing behind the curtain squeezing Poppy Rocco's gold Christ-head emblem my grandmother had given me after he died while waiting anxiously to take my place on stage when Maestro Ricciardi placed his strong reassuring hand on my shoulder and assured me all would be great and to sing from my heart which he knew I did well.

"Act one began at 8:02 p.m. and I could feel the energy in the theater and the artistic chemistry between me and Jonathan Di Lorenzo as friends was off the charts! I was delighted to learn that my former voice competition rival was now going to be my onstage friend and esteemed colleague in La Bohème my all-time favorite opera!

"I also got to sing with Rita Del Angel a Mexican soprano with whom I had wonderful musical onstage

154

chemistry and to this day we are still good friends. The moment of truth had finally arrived when I sang *Che Gelida Manina, Rodolfo's aria,* at the risk of sounding overly confident I honestly felt I was in great voice, the sound was open with a beautiful dark ringing buzzing sound. This is one of the rare times I will ever compliment myself, but I felt everything had fallen into place for me that night. I received very warm and exciting applause from the audience and Rita was equally and even more well-received than I and certainly was very happy for her.

"As Act three came and went, I was on cruise control and felt I had finally hit my stride as a singer. I was so happy and humbled by the experience that when I went into my dressing room I kneeled and thanked the Lord for His goodness and love for me," said Sebastian humbly.

"Mr. Devereux, can you please explain further what you meant by being humbled? I would think you would be pleased and happy by what you accomplished that night?" asked Matthew inquisitively.

"Oh, please don't misunderstand me as I was very happy, but I would say I was also humbled and in awe of where I was that night and more importantly 'Who' truly made it possible for me. You see, Matthew, we are nothing without God. I don't mean to sound preachy, but it has to be said that we have what we have as human beings is because of God.

"I was always slow in everything and nothing has come easily for me and if I have what I have it is because of God who gave me the strength and wisdom to work hard and develop my craft as a singer," said Sebastian piously.

Matthew smiled politely and changed the subject to inquire as to where Sebastian's career had taken him next.

"Well, Jonathan embraced me hard as he said I sang more beautifully that night than he had ever heard me do before. I was crying at that moment and Rita del Angel my leading soprano embraced me and I kissed her hand complimenting her angelic voice similar to that of Renata Tebaldi, and she carried herself in that same fashion.

"Shortly afterward, my family and friends came backstage to congratulate me on my huge success, and I was surprised to receive that level of praise from my family especially my aunt Shirley as she was a perfectionist and didn't pay idle compliments to anyone as she made you earn her words of praise. I guess it is from being an editor-in-chief of a publishing company that trained her to read and evaluate critically. My mom was happy and kissed me on my forehead like she used to do when I was nine years old and brought home a great report card from school.

"Grandmama smiled at me in a way you could tell was genuinely proud of her grandson Seby. She leaned in to kiss me on my cheek and said '*I told you, You could do it!*' signifying that I ought not to fear that it was too late for me and that night was living proof I had started a brand new future doing something I truly loved and was destined to do," said Sebastian.

Matthew continued to write as Sebastian explained where his career was now headed.

"After my enormous success with La Bohème, I was now headed to Europe and my first stop was to sing at the San Carlo opera where I reprised my role as Rodolfo for their 2011–2012 season. It was a new experience for me as I didn't know what to expect as I was greeted by both warmth and praise from the Italian audiences. I was not fluent but had a working knowledge of the Italian language and practiced it more living there for that season.

"The people and food were wonderful and even made friends with some of the native Italians from that region and people who came from Tuscany and other regions to see the performances of La Bohème. Maestro Ricciardi also guests conducted there for me in several performances," said Sebastian.

"So, after your success at the San Carlo Opera where did your success take you next?" asked Matthew.

"I then flew northeast to the grand elegant musical city of Vienna! I was in awe at the prospect of singing at the Vienna State Opera where opera is taken very seriously! Have you ever been to Vienna? It is a charming and lovely city adorned with magical and beautiful castles, museums, cafes, theaters like *The Burg Theater* also known as *the Imperial court theater* stages from the finest plays and dramas. I would often ride on the *Strassen Bahn* and see it on my right-hand side as I purposely sat on the right side of the streetcar so as to get a good look at it!

"But for me, nothing was as majestic as the Wiener Staatsoper, *the Vienna State Opera*, and at night, it looked like a shimmering jewelry box adorned with beautiful strobing street lights projecting against this illustrious landmark of Viennese culture and grand high art. Some say

Vienna is not as exciting as Paris, but if I had to choose, I'd choose Vienna for its beautiful history and affinity for music and culture. I would say she has a quiet but distinct elegance and is every singer's dream to be called to sing in her concert halls and opera house.

"I sang Alfredo in La Traviata for my season there and I truly enjoyed the learning experience and comradery I felt performing for the Austrians. Sadly, after my time was ending there I experienced homesickness so my mother flew to Vienna to spend some time with me so I'd feel less alone and after my short time in Hamburg, Germany where I sang a dozen performances of Nemorino from The Elixir of Love by Donizetti my contract with Europe was finally over and Mom and I decided to fly to Israel!" said Sebastian joyfully.

"Wow! Why Israel of all places?" asked Matthew.

"My mother and I had always dreamed of visiting *The Holy Land* and wanted to have that *Bucket List* experience together. We traveled from Berlin to Tel Aviv and upon approaching the coastline of Tel Aviv from the Mediterranean Sea, we could see a radiating orangish-blue light radiating from the sunset as we landed in the evening. Mom and I looked at each other in sheer amazement as we landed in the land of our God!

"As we were approaching Tel Aviv, I immediately took out my cell phone and filmed a brief video of our landing at Ben Gurion airport like most people do and upload it to YouTube nowadays. We stayed in a beautiful hotel in Tel-Aviv overlooking the Mediterranean and upon being received by the concierge, Mom and I were treated like

royalty and given a fabulous suite equipped with all the trappings offered to only celebrities.

"For the first three days, we bathed in the Mediterranean and enjoyed sightseeing all around the city, but I knew it wouldn't be too long before Mom would become restless and want to visit Jerusalem, the main reason for our visit. Our new good friends at the hotel arranged for a special private tour to Jerusalem and we were flown on Israir to Eliat and then driven all around Jerusalem as I had been gaining recognition as a young famous tenor throughout the USA and Europe.

"We saw the Wailing Wall, the Holocaust Museum, the Church of the Holy Sepulcher in Jerusalem, and at that moment, we finally understood what it meant to be a Christian. We had traveled to: 'our' own Mecca and no place where we had visited before could ever come close to the euphoria and holiness we experienced in Jerusalem. This was a vacation we would never forget and we also cemented new friendships with a lovely couple in their late 50s named Ari and Muriel. They treated us so kindly as they knew we were from the United States and I suppose it didn't hurt that Mom carried a small Israeli flag with her everywhere we walked throughout Jerusalem," said Sebastian jokingly.

"Was that vacation in Israel a spiritual pilgrimage for you and your mother?" asked Matthew.

"It most certainly was in every way imaginable and it was truly lovely to have met that lovely couple. I even made friends with Ari and Muriel's children who were a bit younger than me.

"My mother had a wonderful time talking to their parents reiterating her support for Israel and conveying her happiness at the declaration of Jerusalem as the eternal capital of Israel by the United States. They smiled enthusiastically and offered Mom more food and beverage, but my mom was not the type to overstay her welcome but did accept a little more wine after the wonderful meal they prepared for us, but we then had to prepare for our journey back to Tel-Aviv. We said our goodbye to our new friends and I even exchanged cell# and I friended my new friends on Instagram as that is one of the only social media outlets I now use.

"Mom and I went back to our hotel in Tel Aviv and enjoyed the last few days of our 2-week excursion and then flew back to the United States as my contract tour was up in Europe and wanted to spend time with my family, especially Grandmama as my aunt Shirley told me via WhatsApp that she was slowing down and ailing and very much wanted to see us," said Sebastian sadly.

"Did you get to spend time with your grandmother before she died? Did she get to see you perform before she died?" asked Matthew.

"As a matter of fact, she did and the whole family did everything they could to make Grandmama's remaining time with us a happy one. Mom and I went to visit Grandmama at the apartment where she was living alone and after we all greeted each other, she sat down and looked at us with a look of profound sadness and said to us she was dying. We could not believe what she was telling us and in such a chillingly serene way.

"At that moment, I was moving around in my chair and felt restless and wanted to flee this painful scene, but Mom whispered to me to calm myself as Grandmama needed us now. We stayed with her for the rest of the afternoon and left around 10 p.m. so she would feel less alone.

"We ordered take-out and dined together as a family, in a way we hadn't been accustomed to in quite a long time," said Sebastian as he started crying and Matthew offered him a tissue and looked at him compassionately.

"What did you all do for your grandmother? What was wrong with her medically?" asked Matthew with concern.

"Grandmama had been diagnosed with Stage three colon cancer and the irony for me was that she took such good care of herself. She was an avid walker and followed a strict diet and never allowed herself to gain weight, but I guess gravity eventually takes its toll on everyone including Grandmama who I thought would live forever.

"I guess we see our loved ones as we wish to see them and when they succumb to their own mortality, it shakes our world to utter destruction. She lived for another seven months and in that time my aunt Shirley, mom, and I did our best to try and help Grandmama enjoy what was left during her time on earth," said Sebastian resolutely.

"Did your grandmother get to watch you perform before she died?" asked Matthew.

"Fortunately for me, Grandmama had the opportunity to come to watch me perform as Pinkerton in Madame Butterfly in October 2014, and it was a beautiful performance as I sang with two of my favorite colleagues; Rita del Angel and Jonathan Di Lorenzo. They knew what I was going through as I confided in them with all of my

deepest pain in dealing with soon losing Grandmama. They were completely supportive of me and after the performance, they brought Grandmama backstage to meet the performers and she was on Cloud nine being a part of the wonderful world of opera. Grandmama also came to one performance of me performing as Ruggero from the Puccini operetta *La Rondine.*

"It was such an exciting but also a bittersweet debut for me because Grandmama was becoming thinner and more sickly and needed assistance the entire time she was present, but thankfully, she did make it to the Saturday matinee performance in March 2015, and I really performed with great intensity in my role as Ruggero.

"Fortunately, Maestro Ricciardi conducted for my debut performance and he gave me the confidence and strength I needed to perform at my optimal best because that afternoon I sang for a woman who had sacrificed and loved her family wholeheartedly in every sense of the word. I just wanted to give a little back to her on stage and I think she knew it because as I looked out at the side Grand Tier box I could see her smiling with her eyes as I sang my arias, duets, and the famous Act two quartet song called *Bevo al tuo fresco sorriso* which generated such intense energy within me that knowing Grandmama was present only added to the excitement and melancholy that coexisted within me.

"I told myself before I went out on stage that I had to make this performance a great one because I knew there would be no do-over as Grandmama would probably not be able to leave her home after that day. I had to work on convincing my aunt Shirley to agree to let Grandmama attend this performance and Mom was also very helpful in

this joint effort, but Grandmama, fortunately, cast the deciding vote and was determined to be present whether she felt well enough or not.

"After the performance, I approached her, and she cupped my face with her hands and told me that she loved my performance and that she would be watching over me and my singing career. At that moment, I held back my tears, composed myself and we took Grandmama home to spend the evening with her at her apartment while eating takeout and playing Pavarotti arias and Whitney Houston's greatest hits to make her feel more at home among family," said Sebastian tearfully.

"So, was that *Rondine* performance truly the last time she watched you perform on stage?" asked Matthew.

"Sadly, yes it was the last time she saw me perform on stage because two weeks later she was taken to the hospital and after an extensive check-up she was sent to a hospice to pass her remaining time in the company of her loved ones and caring nurses who tended to her needs.

"I remember that even in Grandmama's state of being, she still charmed and cheered the nurses, doctors, and hospice administrators with her wonderful sense of humor and strong opinions. Grandmama was definitely highly-opinionated, but she was truly genuine and very good-hearted," said Sebastian lamentably.

"Did you get to spend time with your grandmother at the hospice and communicate your thoughts with her?" asked Matthew.

"Tragically, mom, Rachel, and I only got to see her a few times because my father came up from Florida to spend some time with her and we could not be in the same room

together. My aunt Shirley told me he couldn't believe that Grandmama was very sick, but when he saw her, he realized that it was true and tried to spend quality time with her.

"I understand their time together alone was precious; I certainly hope so as he had not spoken to her for a long time before she became ill. I was very sad that I could not be with her as she was ailing, but I understood that she needed to be with her son and if I loved her, I needed to understand this, and I certainly did! The last time we saw her was the day before Mother's Day and the three of us spent the afternoon with her and when she saw me, she didn't know who I was, but she recognized my mom and Rachel, I was sad but understood it wasn't her fault.

"She would awake and then fall asleep and then reawake. I fed her water through a straw and it was the most precious thing that happened between us as I remember she took care of me as a child when I was sick. She once nursed me back to health when we were driving home from Florida to New York. I was burning up with fever, and we were staying in a small town in North Carolina overnight, she was determined to nurse me back to health and she put cold compresses with rubbing alcohol almost every hour, and when morning approached, she took my temperature at 6 a.m.

"My temperature went from 102 to 98.4 and triumphantly helped me to sponge bath and get dressed for the second leg of our journey home. Grandmama made sure I ate and drank apple juice so I wouldn't have a fever relapse and on the drive home I was more talkative as I always was when I was with Grandmama and Poppy Rocco. I love and miss them both so much," said Sebastian sadly.

"We spent the whole afternoon with Grandmama, but we knew it was time to say our goodbyes so Mom and Rachel went first and I then asked them to wait outside for me so I could say goodbye to Grandmama in my own personal way, I sang a Spanish Zarzuela aria called *No Puede Ser* which was her favorite Spanish aria. She was very weak at this point, but she listened to me sing and drank it with pleasure.

"For me, that was the ultimate seal of approval I needed and received from Grandmama. I kissed her goodbye and a few days later she passed away peacefully. At her memorial service at the U.S. Veteran's cemetery, we said prayers for her and then played Luciano Pavarotti's *Nessun Dorma* which we played on Grandmama's boom box, and fortunately, Rachel recorded it on her cell phone. I remember the cry of Vincero which means I will win in Italian and as far as I was concerned, Grandmama was a winner in so many ways, and I was privileged to have known, loved, and been loved by this powerful woman," said Sebastian bittersweetly.

"Was your father at your grandmother's memorial service?" asked Matthew.

"Oh, yes, he was there, but out of respect for Grandmama's memory, he stayed in his place and I did the same. I won't say it was easy being in an awkward situation like sharing the same space with my estranged father, but all things considered, I think we did splendidly. So now Matthew, we are now here that should bring you up to speed on my life," said Sebastian.

"Well, let's take a break, and afterward, I would like to ask you some lightning round questions on your family,

future singing projects, and faith," said Matthew triumphantly.

Chapter 13

At this point during the interview, Sebastian and Matthew had relaxed more as they both sensed that the more difficult parts of the interview had now come to an end and this was Sebastian's opportunity to tighten up any loose ends between Sebastian and some of the people and topics he deeply cared about. It was now about 9:30 p.m., but neither man seemed willing to wrap up the interview just yet.

"Mr. Devereux, we certainly have discussed some very deep topics involving your family, childhood, and operatic career. I'd like to ask you some questions about your family first. You've addressed some, what I would imagine are, painful memories of certain individuals in your family, can you name some pleasant memories of these individuals beginning with your father?" asked Matthew.

"Absolutely, I would say I have beautiful simple memories such as when I was four years old my father would smoke his pipe in the living room and I would peek my head out to hear the WWOR TV late night bumper playing in the background while he was smoking his late night pipe.

"It was such a pleasant combination of sound and smell. He would then smile and motion me to come over to him and let me sit on his lap and we'd watch the movie together until I fell asleep. I also remember us sharing a deli sandwich together while we would talk about life. I'd ask him about his law practice and he would smile because I took a genuine interest in his practice and he would then ask me about school and my social life. My father also introduced me to the exciting world of classic movies like *Ben-Hur*, *Taras Bulba* and *The Big Country* among others. I remember my father once took me alone to Amish country and we ate at Hershey Farms smorgasbord. We had a very nice stress-free time. It truly was one of the few times I felt at peace with my father and he really catered to me and made me feel important. We behaved like two adult men sharing our lives' stories and it really is a shame that we couldn't have been closer because we both would have really enriched each other's lives as adults but sadly, I believe my father's insecurity and jealousy ruined that forever.

"Sadly, we didn't have many happy moments together, but the ones we did share did have an impact on me. My father James was a very hardworking man and an excellent lawyer and musician with a great deal of intelligence and passion for his work and art. He could be a compassionate man and help his friends who were in trouble and he also helped his family when they needed legal advice, but since he was short-tempered, he could sadly take out his anger on innocent people who never meant him any harm. I have come to the point where I have learned to forgive him as I

realize he often lashed out at us from a place of pain and insecurity.

"Moreover, I pray for him all the time and ask God to bless him and his wife; Consuelo, to be happy and healthy. I realize you sometimes have to love some people from a distance, and I believe God took my father out of my life for His own reasons and resigned myself to accept that a long time ago," said Sebastian peacefully.

"It sounds to me that you have moved on in regard to your father. I'm glad to hear it and it certainly has served you well in life," declared Matthew.

"Thank you, I am now in a very good place emotionally and artistically and I have incorporated those painful childhood memories into my art and interpreting the roles I have sung in my career. I have now come to believe that we cannot always prevent difficult circumstances from happening, but we can allow these same difficult circumstances to strengthen and purify us," said Sebastian retrospectively.

"What are some of the good traits of your mother's ex-husband Javier Mauricio?" asked Matthew.

"This one is not as easy for me to answer, but I will say that he can be very generous with people especially people who are in trouble but sometimes with resources of other people. He would sometimes give money or things to other people but many times at the expense of my mother. I remember a time when Javier's mother Eduvina wanted to send kitchen utensils to her family in Colombia and asked for help, so he immediately volunteered to give away our kitchen utensils.

"When my mother, rightly, protested this idea, he overreacted childishly, and then his mother started to cry and asked Javier to take her home as she didn't expect my mother to react this way. He could be helpful and even try to bring people together in very unconventional ways like he tried to do between my father and me, but sadly, it blew up in everyone's face. As resentful as I was toward Javier for a very long time, I have slowly begun to forgive him for how he mistreated mom, Rachel, and me and ask God to bless him," said Sebastian pensively.

"What are some of the good traits of Warren?" asked Matthew.

"Well, Warren and I did not interact with each other nearly as long as I did with the others you mentioned, but he could be funny, charming, and even generous when he wanted to be. He was never much for deep discussion, but at times like the times we went out to dinner, he would talk about us living together in an apartment and live near my mom so we could be a family together, but as nice as those ideas sounded, there was something deep within me that always knew he was just joking with me and I put it out of my mind. Warren was my best friend for a while, and I will always enjoy that special time in my life, but it ended when it needed to and I wish him well," said Sebastian.

"Can you tell me anything good about Mrs. Tarantella?" asked Matthew.

"Sadly, I can tell you very little that was good about her, but one good thing that happened was that I visited her in a nursing home in Suffern, N.Y. where she was staying many years later.

"Naturally, she didn't know who I was, but I made sure she became very well acquainted with me by the time I was through having my say! I told her how much she had hurt and humiliated me while I was in her class and hoped she had never done anything like that to any other student, but she vaguely remembered what happened to me while I was a pupil of hers. I did not allow that to deter me and told her that as angry as I was with her for torturing me the way she did, I still forgave her and wished her all the best.

"She looked at me bewildered and stunned, but she then realized who I was and did apologize to me and said she had always regretted not having been able to issue that apology to me years earlier, but I had already left St. Robert's by that time. I was finally at peace with myself and we had a nice chat for the next hour.

"As I was about to say goodbye, she touched my hand and said she wished me all the best in my singing career after I filled her in on my work while in the Met opera chorus. I left having felt freer than I had been in many years as I had finally faced a huge demon that day! She passed away a couple of years later, but I am so glad I finally had that time to deal with that important piece of unfinished business," said Sebastian triumphantly.

"What were some of the good traits about your mother and grandmother?" asked Matthew.

"Well, my mom, Vanessa has always been strong, loving and she has always believed in me and my educational and artistic aspirations. Getting a good education has always been paramount for her, but she has also believed in my pursuing what makes me happy and when I shared with her my desire to sing, she understood

completely and gave me her complete moral support and admiration for having the fortitude to pursue higher education in getting my bachelor's degree in creative writing and English and my master's degree in Spanish.

"Both Mom and Poppy Rocco were in complete agreement about that! I have not always agreed with every decision my mom has made in her life and at times we have disagreed passionately, but at the end of the day, we see eye to eye on the most important issues and I have always loved and supported Mom for being my mom and I could never have asked God for a better mom than she was to me.

"As for Grandmama, she was a wonderful, strong, and loving mother and grandmother and I will always place her on a pedestal even with her imperfections because let's face it, we all have them. I thank the Lord for having blessed me with an amazing woman like Grandmama Rita and consider it a great privilege for having had her in my life for as long I had. I just pray she is finally at peace and watching over me from Heaven," said Sebastian proudly but sadly.

"Alright, let's switch gears and discuss your favorite operatic roles and singers whom you have admired over the years," said Matthew.

"I have always admired many of the great tenors from the 1950s, 1960s, and 1970s mostly such as Di Stefano, Bergonzi, Corelli, Björling, Gedda, Merrill, Tebaldi, Callas, Price, Arroyo, Pavarotti, Domingo, and of course Carreras and would listen to each of these wonderful artists to gleam what I could to help guide me in my own singing, but I always returned to Carreras without fail. I guess it is because I admired his sensitivity and arresting intensity of delivery when he sang. He may not have had the largest

tenor voice, but it was, nevertheless, quite beautiful and it communicated deep and heartfelt emotion whenever I would sing along with his recordings especially his recordings of 1970s.

"I also greatly admired whenever Carreras sang with the legendary Montserrat Caballẽ, it was always a treat to hear those two sing Donizetti, Verdi, and Puccini. I have also admired the famous Pearl Fishers duet sung by Björling and Merrill as their interpretation has served as the gold standard for how that duet should be sung! I have also admired Maria Callas' Casta Diva from the opera Norma and Vissi d'Arte from Puccini's Tosca, Renata Tebaldi's Senza Mamma from Puccini's opera Suor Angelica among others as vocal arias and duets which have really moved me to tears.

"As far as instrumental pieces, I love Chopin preludes and Rachmaninoff's piano concerto# 3 and Tchaikovsky's piano concerto because both pieces move me to fear and hope and everything in between," said Sebastian.

"What does your Christian faith mean to you?" asked Matthew reverently.

"My Christian faith has been a joyful and difficult journey at times. I'd compare it to a seesaw at times as one's walk with the Lord does not always move in a straight line but a zigzag formation; however, I believe the Lord brings His children where they need to be. I had a great deal of lessons to learn especially in the areas of forgiveness, patience, and determination to not give up whenever our thoughts and fears often scream at us to do just that! In my Christian walk, I have much to learn and am a work in progress but I do tell you that my faith in God gives me

strength not just in my singing career but also in my personal life."

"The Lord has shown me that He will never leave me nor forsake me even if all others abandon me as I had been by certain individuals in my life. I am and have everything I have today because of God and try to share my faith through my music whether I am singing opera or oratorio which is a Christian form of opera set to singing without background sets," said Sebastian.

"What future singing projects are you hoping to work on in the coming years?" asked Matthew.

"I am now hoping to work on singing more French operas, some more Italian operas like lighter Verdi and Donizetti as well as a couple of more Puccini operas. I am also now looking to return to musical theater and make some studio recordings of *Sound of Music*, *King and I*, *West Side Story*, *Candide*, and *South Pacific*. I also hope to return to comprimario roles once I have completed my pending contracts with the Met, Vienna State Opera, San Carlo, Rome, and London's Covent Garden within the next five years.

"I have been extremely blessed Matthew and would not change a thing in how my career turned out only to say that if all I had sung was in the chorus and comprimario tenor work then I would have been quite content, but the Lord has been very good to me in allowing me to have enjoyed this chapter in my life and as a form of gratitude I would also love to record some oratorios such as Handel's Messiah and record some sacred songs by both Catholic and protestant composers," said Sebastian humbly.

"To quote Bernard Pivot, if Heaven exists, what would you like to hear God say when you arrive at the pearly gates?" asked Matthew shockingly.

"I told you Sebastian that I would always love and take care of you. Well done, good and faithful servant," said Sebastian smilingly.

"Thank you so much for your generosity of spirit in sharing your life with me and my readers! Thank you for being a true scholar and artist. Most importantly, thank you for trusting me with the most vulnerable and important part of your life, your early childhood, and that of your family as well as your artistry and faith.

"You really have shared a rich part of your life and shall do my very best to not betray you with writing your biography. I shall be very careful in safeguarding your life story so that it will be presented in an honorable way for all my readers to learn from and enjoy. Thank you, Sebastian Devereux, Congratulations on a life well-lived!" said Matthew with great admiration.

At this point, both Sebastian and Matthew had concluded their interview, and Matthew shared what would happen as he wrote Sebastian's biography and what to expect after its release.

"So what are your plans now that we have finished the interview? What are you going to do going forward?" asked Matthew.

"I am going to fly down to be with my mom tomorrow afternoon and spend a week with her in our home in Sarasota and then I have to return to resume rehearsals for

our charity concert at the end of the month. I need a rest from everything I've been dealing with especially the death of Grandmama. I hope the book will be a huge success for you and that your readers will enjoy it as much as I enjoyed being a part of it," said Sebastian.

"Thank you, I will be in touch within the next few months after its completion and publication," said Matthew intellectually.

"Has anyone ever told you that you look like Bradley Cooper?" said Sebastian smilingly and a bit flirtatiously.

"No, nobody ever has but you. I'm flattered by the compliment," said Matthew blushingly.

"Well, it certainly has been a pleasure, Mr. Porter, and thank you for keeping your promise to me in making sure this interview would be painless because you made me feel as if I were talking with a good friend... on my terms. For this, I am truly thankful, and I wish you all the best in your future writing projects," said Sebastian.

Both Sebastian and Matthew shook hands and hugged each other in a brotherly way, and Matthew left Sebastian's apartment with all that he had learned about Sebastian Devereux a man who had won against all odds and a low bar line set by all of his doubters. Sebastian called the airline to book a ticket to Sarasota on a Sunday 2 p.m. flight and then left a message for Mrs. Alba leaving a voice mail message telling her he'd be away and would return home with his mother the following weekend.

"Hi, mom, hope all is well I know you are out but just wanted to tell you I am flying down to meet you in Sarasota

and hope you can meet me at the airport tomorrow afternoon as I just made a plane reservation and will arrive in Sarasota at around 4:30. Call me when you can to let me know you got this message. Love you, mom. Bye," said Sebastian happily.

Chapter 14

Sebastian did fly down to Sarasota that following day and spent a week with his mother, aunt Valeria and Mom's dear friend, Alexis, came over from her home in Northport to spend some time visiting with the family. Whenever Sebastian did not feel like going to the nearby UT mall or outlet stores, he would spend time in trekking, cycling, and walking around his community and of course rehearsing for his upcoming charity concert he was participating in with five of his other singing colleagues including Jonathan Di Lorenzo and Maria del Angel. After much-needed rest, Sebastian and his mother returned home that Saturday afternoon.

"Home sweet home! Are you glad to be home, mom?" asked Sebastian.

"Yes, for now. I really enjoy our time in Florida, but it is good to travel back and forth. Are you ready to go back to rehearsal on Tuesday?" asked Vanessa with concern.

"Yes, I think I am... in fact, I know I am. This biography interview helped me to put things in my life in perspective and Matthew Porter was great at doing it in a way that was non-threatening to me. I just hope he writes a

best seller and that his readers will enjoy it. Mom, not to change the subject but why not invite your friend Norma to the apartment for Sunday brunch. She's such a good friend to you and it would be nice to see her," said Sebastian enthusiastically.

"Oh, alright, that would be very nice, but I'll have to call her and see if she is available. Maybe we can ask Mrs. Alba to come by to prepare brunch for us and as soon as we're done, she can go home right after she cleans up. I wouldn't want her to lose her whole day off and we'd certainly pay her double time for tomorrow," said Vanessa.

"Okay, call Norma first and see if she'll be available to come tomorrow for brunch and if she says yes, I'll call Mrs. Alba and ask her to work a few hours tomorrow," said Sebastian.

Norma agreed to come over for brunch at 12 p.m., and Mrs. Alba was more than happy to collaborate because she missed Sebastian and his mother, and it would be a good way to see them and make a little extra money in the process. Norma came over to the apartment and arrived at 11:45 a.m. while Vanessa was getting ready to come out, but before she did that, she needed to make sure she was properly dressed, makeup had to be just right and her "helmet hair" in a state of complete perfection… anything less would simply not do.

"Hi, Norma! How are you? Welcome to our home please come in," said Sebastian warmly.

"Hi, Sebastian! Thank you for the lovely invitation! How was your flight home from Sarasota? Did you both

have a good time spending time away from New York? I missed you both," said Norma warmly.

"Well, Mom certainly had a great time and when I told her I was going to join her in Sarasota she was very happy about it and we made the most of our time away together. Let's go to the living room and sit down while we wait for Mom and Mrs. Alba to let us know that brunch is ready. She went to the market early this morning and has been cooking since 10:30 a.m. She's amazing! So how is Giorgio your boyfriend and your beautiful family?" asked Sebastian with concern.

"Oh, he's fine thanks for asking, and my little grandson, Robby is getting big and playing sports and is doing very well in school and my son Patrick is doing well too. How is your concert coming along, your mom has been telling me all about it?" asked Norma.

At that precise moment, Vanessa followed by Mrs. Alba came out to greet Norma with a warm embrace and with the grand announcement that brunch was ready and should be seated to a beautiful buffet-style brunch consisting of eggs, sausage, Canadian bacon, hash browns, fruit, silver dollar-pancakes, and brisket of beef. When Mrs. Alba cooked, no detail was too small. Norma was delighted and complimented Mrs. Alba, but in typical fashion, she humbly accepted the compliment and then excused herself to the kitchen to allow Sebastian, Vanessa, and Norma to enjoy their brunch and conversation peacefully.

"Sebastian, how is your rehearsal coming along? I can't wait to watch you perform on August 29. Giorgio and I will

be there, and of course, your mother will also be there," said Norma rhetorically.

"Yes, I am ready. It was difficult initially as I was struggling with Grandmama just recently passing away, but I feel she has given me the confidence from Heaven I needed to assure me all would be well and should continue to go about life as usual. I resume my rehearsals on Tuesday with Maestro Ricciardi," said Sebastian.

"Oh, yes, Seby was struggling a lot, especially at the cemetery. Did you know he played Mama Rita's favorite aria, *Nessun Dorma* sung by Pavarotti at the service? The energy in the tent where the service was held had a powerful magnetism and you should have seen what was happening! James, Sebastian's father, lost his cell phone right outside of the cemetery office/gate and Sebastian's uncle Jeff, the cell phone wasn't working at all. Luckily, Rachel filmed the recording of *Nessun Dorma*, so Sebastian was able to save and upload it to his YouTube channel after we came home from the cemetery.

"I could actually picture Rita conducting with her hands to the aria and Seby had the aria playing at full volume for effect! It was a beautiful service and fortunately, James found his cell phone once we got near the gate of the cemetery and he didn't even look at us nor did we look at him to keep peace in the family. As we were leaving the cemetery gate a song came on the radio called *Gloria* sung by Laura Branigan and the reason that was significant because Rita's guardian angel's name was Gloria and we felt that was her way of telling us she was fine," said Vanessa tearfully.

"Wow, that is quite a story! I'm glad everything turned out fine though and that Rita had a beautiful service accompanied by that beautiful aria which I have heard many times sung by Pavarotti! He was an amazing singer! Giorgio has several of his albums at home," said Norma.

The three of them had a wonderful afternoon together eating and watching movies on Netflix together and Norma left around 7 p.m. with a smile on her face after having had such a lovely time with Vanessa and Sebastian and sent them a text to thank them.

Tuesday was finally here, and Sebastian marched right back to rehearsal and had a new resolve to sing as he had never sung before. Maestro Ricciardi welcomed Sebastian with a warm embrace and spoke to Sebastian to make sure all was fine and the results spoke for themselves because Sebastian was right where his story begun, but he sang *Federico's Lament*; *E La Solita Storia* with a fresh, open, and dark, but warm lyric sound and truly became the part of a lamenting young shepherd male who cried because the person whom he loved was taken away.

After the end of the aria, Maestro Ricciardi and orchestra gave Sebastian rousing applause and standing ovation which was very rare and difficult to get but Sebastian humbly and gratefully accepted the warm reception he received from the present company. Sebastian and Jonathan later sang Pearl Fisher's duet and again both were very warmly applauded for their performance.

Finally, August 29 performance night was here, and the Lincoln Center Avery Fisher Hall was filled to capacity and

all the performers including Sebastian had sung their arias and duets and received very warm applause and cheers of BRAVO echoing throughout the entire hall. Now came the encores, Jonathan sang the *Toreador Song* from Carmen, Maria del Angel sang *Senza Mamma* from Suor Angelica and Sebastian sang *Nessun Dorma* to close the concert and nobody, but Maestro Ricciardi and Sebastian knew of this and Sebastian was quite nervous as he sang all the familiar stanzas he had heard Pavarotti and other interpreters of this aria sing over the years, but he had the resolve to sing this for his Grandmama Rita. Finally, he came to that stanza… al 'alba Vincero… Vincero… VINCERO!

Sebastian Devereux was greeted by thunderous applause and a 15-minute standing ovation and once all the other performers came out on stage the ovation and cheers lasted for another 45 minutes! It was a magical and surreal evening for Sebastian that night.

Six months had passed, and Sebastian was at home alone because Vanessa went out with her friend Norma to a museum followed by dinner. The doorbell rang and it was a familiar voice at the other end of the door, it was Matthew Porter.

"Wow! Matthew what a pleasant and unexpected surprise! Won't you come in?" asked Sebastian.

"Thank you, Mr. Devereux. Please don't be upset that your doorman didn't announce me as I asked him to not announce me because I wanted to surprise you. I won't detain you, but I wanted to tell you I saw your concert on television six months ago and I have to say I was so moved by your beautiful voice and you really had me chocked up when you sang your arias and that gorgeous Friendship duet

from the Pearl Fishers. I have to say though, your powerful rendition of *Nessun Dorma* was truly a tour de force! You were spectacular and after I watched that concert, I knew I had interviewed the right vocalist for my book, and speaking of books look what I brought you!" declared Matthew proudly while he handed Sebastian an autographed copy of *Sebastian Devereux; On My Terms.*

"Wow! I like it... a catchy title too! And it's autographed to me.... will this make it harder for me to exchange if I don't like it?" asked Sebastian playfully.

Matthew at first looked startled, but Sebastian admitted he was joking and playfully jabbed him in the arm.

"I was only joking Matthew and please call me Sebastian, I now consider you a good friend who has done my life justice in ways unimaginable. I know I haven't read it yet, but I have a strong instinct about these things. Thank you, my dear friend, for bringing this to me. I shall treasure it always and will remember our time together while reading it," said Sebastian proudly.

As Matthew was about to leave Sebastian touched his shoulder and asked him if he'd like to have coffee or dinner with him socially.

"Wow, I wasn't expecting that but sure, why not? It would be great to pick up where we left off now as friends instead of business acquaintances," said Matthew flirtatiously smiling at Sebastian, as he opened the door to leave, Sebastian hugged Matthew warmly while Matthew playfully touched Sebastian's wavy hair, cupped his face and kissed him sweetly first on his lips then on his forehead.

Both men smiled at each other while Sebastian blushes and Matthew smiled, winked, and closed the door behind him. There was a growing sense that this was only the beginning of something special blooming between both Sebastian and Matthew which caused Sebastian to leap for joy in his heart.

At that moment, Sebastian walked over to his stereo console and turned on his stereo to play Pavarotti's Nessun Dorma as he pondered some of the original questions, he asked himself at the beginning of his story such as who he was, what career to choose, what would he do differently? As Sebastian walked out on his enclosed terrace and beheld the sunshine shining from Manhattan, he realized at that moment that he was destined to do exactly what he was doing and wouldn't change a thing and as that same last phrase al 'alba vincero... Vincero... Vincero played resplendently as he meditated on Pavarotti's 1978 recording of that aria realizing he had already won in every way a man could win.

"Sebastian Devereux, you are truly a blessed man, and may God and all of His wonderful blessings continue to be with me as I live, love, and sing well. May I be at peace in every pertinent area of my life and may I continue to grow as a man and as an artist," Sebastian said to himself aloud.

Shortly afterward, Sebastian's iPhone rang as a new text came through and it was a message from Matthew telling Sebastian how much he enjoyed interviewing him and concluded with a reference to how much he is looking forward to getting to know him better socially and ended his text with emoticons of a few hugs, a kiss, and a wink face. At that moment, Sebastian was beside himself but regained

his composure and replied with a hug and kiss emoticon and ended the text with a simple Ditto and wink. Shortly afterward, Sebastian's iPhone rang, and it was Jonathan on the other end.

"Hi, Jonathan, how are you? Do I have a lot to tell you!" said Sebastian smiling to himself while he sat down on his patio recliner on his terrace.

The End